LT-No

THE PERALTA
COUNTRY

Also by Richard Clarke
THE HOMESTEADERS
THE COPPERDUST HILLS

THE PERALTA COUNTRY

Richard Clarke

Walker and Company
New York

First published in the United States of America
in 1987 by the Walker Publishing Company, Inc.

Published simultaneously in Canada by John Wiley & Sons Canada, Limited, Rexdale, Ontario.

Printed in the United States of America

10 9 8 7 6 5 4 3 2 1

Library of Congress Cataloging-in-Publication Data

Richard Clarke
   The Peralta country.

   I. Title.
PS3566.A34P4   1987   813'.54   86-28971
ISBN 0-8027-0949-4

Contents

CHAPTER 1
Shades of Autumn

THE softwoods remained dark green, uneven swatches of summer-color surrounded and infiltrated by the hardwoods, whose leaves were turning with the soft breath of oncoming autumn—russet, gold, cordovan brown, amethyst—ready to fall with the first breath of cold wind.

From a distance, the tawny foothills with their carpeting of stirrup-high curing grass rippled with each groundswell breeze that flowed southward across open range all the way to the town of Peralta. The foothills shone dull tan against the backdrop of higher hills, and farther northward, there were crumpled mountains of enormous bulk. The farther up one looked, the less one saw of any color except dark green; hardwoods did not prosper at the greater heights.

Clouds arrived, usually by stealth in the cooling nights, and hovered over blue-blurred peaks fifty miles from town. If the clouds wore soiled edges, people prophesied an early winter, with ten-foot snowbanks in the mountains and bitterly cold days out over the flat-to-rolling miles of empty grassland.

Rangemen were busy at culling, at making gate-cuts of fat two-year-olds, of anything they did not intend to feed through a winter. There were two busy seasons for rangemen: springtime, when calving was completed and they rode out to mark and brand; autumn, when they rounded up, made their cuts, and organized drives twenty-two miles south to the town of Gloria, where there was a spur track and a large network of shipping corrals.

The days remained hot with a golden half-light. Nights and early mornings were cold. Occasionally Kelly O'Bryon, proprietor of the livery barn at the south end of Peralta, who also did a lot of draying, broke rinds of ice off water troughs and told his hostler—an old, lanky, taciturn man named Bellingham—that autumn, like winter, was "whiskey weather." Old Bellingham said nothing. All kinds of weather were whiskey weather to him. When a man was haunted by memories, whiskey was medicine.

Bellingham was old, whereas Kelly O'Bryon was in his late forties. The old man had been a horse-trader and coach driver, a freighter and hide dealer. Bellingham earned his meager wage, slept in the harness-room under sweat-stiff saddle and horse blankets, wore patched trousers and a ragged old blue shirt, and cast-off boots that were cracked beyond repair. But he had visited the depths, had dwelt there four years. He thought of his employer as a fair man, sometimes too clever for his own good, overfed, a mite lazy, but decent enough.

Bellingham's very private opinion of Kelly was that, as fate occasionally did, it had shielded him from a world turned red and deafening by having him far west of the wide Missouri when everything east of the Missouri had gone berserk. Kelly didn't know anything. Most likely he never would. His world was a simple place of clean air, enormous distances, majestic mountains, horses, cowmen, Peralta.

Bellingham shuffled up to the harness-room for his jacket, something he had found beside the stage road a couple of years earlier. It had holes at the elbows and no buttons, but it was pure wool, which a man needed when those little scuttling ground-level winds stirred dust in the roadway.

Kelly turned back from the alley and the troughs. He had bought seven stacks of wild hay from a settler; his shed was full of firewood. He had seventeen sacks of rolled barley, and the roof didn't leak. He was ready for winter, and to prove it, he sauntered through dust devils in the roadway and hiked northward to the Horseshoe Saloon & Cardroom to visit with the proprietor, a pale, nearly hairless man who shared with

Kelly O'Bryon the distinction of a flabby gut which overrode
the waistband of his britches. The Horseshoe's proprietor
was named Flannery, Pat Flannery. That might be why he
and Kelly got along so well—most of the time. O'Bryon and
Flannery.

Autumn's trumpet—wind—rattled windows, made rooftops give up their summer-long layers of dust. Except for the
log jailhouse with its mighty walls, stone floor, and tiny
barred windows, the wind forced all the wood structures
throughout town to groan and list on fir-log foundations.

The jailhouse office was warm. Too warm, in fact, but it
was almost impossible to build a small fire in the huge old
cast-iron cannon heater near the back wall, a yard or two
north of the gun rack with its slack chain threaded through
triggerguards and locked at one end.

On cold days Constable Walt Cutler's left side ached under
a healed gunshot wound. Doctor Eaton had said the pain
would stop in time, but it hadn't. Walt had been nearly killed
the year before as a result of mistaken identity. He was a
handsome, stalwart man. As Fred Tower, who was not a
small man, had said: Walt Cutler was big enough to eat hay.

The constable sipped hot, black java, vaguely aware of the
fitful wind as he sorted through his mail, found nothing
interesting in it, shoved the wanted dodgers in a low desk
drawer where dozens of other posters were kept, and eventually leaned back, hands behind his head, thinking of the
lady at the cafe. Elizabeth Bartlett had green eyes, red-
auburn hair, a complexion like peaches and cream, and a
slow-healing mourning over her dead husband. It had been
a year, but as Bertha Maloney, who owned the rooming
house, had told him, different kinds of hurt required different periods of healing.

He recalled the nightmare summer of the previous year.
For Elizabeth, the victim of a perverse fate, everything that
would have crushed a strong man had come within an ace of

destroying her faith, her spirit, her will to live. She had lived through it, but, as Bertha had observed, the road back might be a long one. Of course Walt did not have to wait for her; the world was as full of handsome women as the sea was full of fish. Well, maybe not in the sparsely inhabited Peralta country, but it it had been . . . He shifted on the chair, threw an exasperated glare at the popping iron stove, and shook his head. He would wait; what the hell, thirty-five wasn't old.

Lanky Fred Tower came in, bringing wind with him. He closed the door and reset his hat, which he had tugged low to keep it from being carried away. Fred went for the chair along the front wall, unbuttoned his blanket-coat, blew on his big, callused red hands, and said, "What can a man do about wind? Hot weather, well, he finds a lot of shade or maybe a lake in the mountains. Cold weather, he stokes up the stove and wears red underwear. Rain, snow, frost—he can sidle around all of them. But damned wind—he can't work outside when it's blowin', and the darned walls let it in, buildings creak, and shingles fly off. Just what was the good Lord thinkin' of when he concocted wind?"

Walt laughed. "Get a cup off the wall. The coffee's hot."

The harnessmaker did not leave his chair. He pushed back the old coat and thrust long legs out in the direction of the stove. He cocked an ear, then said, "You got the sturdiest buildin' in town. You know that?"

Walt nodded.

Fred had grainy skin, lines, sunken eyes, hands the size of hams, and was leaned down to a nubbin. He was somewhere between fifty and seventy: his type went on and on. He had never been married, and as Walt sat gazing at the older man, he thought that was unfortunate because Fred Tower was the kind of man who made a good husband. There wasn't a selfish bone in his body, he had humor, and while he was not pretty, Walt had seen men with straighter noses and smaller mouths and fewer lines who couldn't have held a candle to Fred Tower for character and just plain decency.

Bertha Maloney, who owned the rooming house, liked him, and that spoke volumes. Bertha had a ramrod up her back, iron in her craw, and wouldn't have lowered her eyes from the devil.

Walt arose and got the coffee for the harnessmaker, silently handed him the cup, and returned to the desk to get comfortable again.

Fred said, "Thanks. Only I ain't crippled." He tasted the coffee. It was too hot, so he put the cup on the corner of Walt's desk to cool as he said, "Gus brought in two saddles and a set of driving harness . . . They'll commence their drive in a week." Fred paused, ran a rummaging glance across the ceiling, cleared his throat, and finally said, "You know old Bellingham?"

Walt nodded. Everyone knew the old scarecrow. "What about him—did he pass out in the roadway again?"

"No. No—someone give him a little brown puppy."

Walt eased his chair down and leaned both thick arms atop the desk. He gazed steadily at Fred. "What about it?"

"That was three days back. Did you see him after that? He was a different man. He made a bed in the harness-room for his dog, got some milk, and warmed it on the woodstove. Kelly told me he acted like it was a little child. He wouldn't even go up to the Horseshoe for a bottle of dregs. He hovered over that little puppy like a mother hen. Old Bellingham even started talking, Kelly said. You know how he's always been; maybe grunted when you talked to him but almost never answered in words. Kelly said he even heard him singing that old Confederate song, *Lorena,* to his puppy in the harness-room." Fred paused to gaze steadily at the town constable, expressionless, motionless, gathering the rest of his recitation into words he chose with care.

Walt knew Fred Tower. He could tell this story was not going to have a nice ending. He half held his breath as he waited.

Fred tasted the coffee. It was still too hot. He gazed from

the lawman to the tips of his scuffed boots. "Puppy died," he said.

Walt let his breath out slowly. "What from?"

"A kick. Busted up his insides."

"Horse or mule?"

"Neither. A man."

Walt did not move or take his eyes off the older man. "How?"

"Well, that pup was real young. He didn't know anyone except old Bellingham. I guess he figured Bellingham was his mother. He'd waddle over to meet him every time he come into the harness-room. You know, puppies always want to eat, and Bellingham always brought him something."

"Fred!"

"I'm gettin' there. Set back, will you? Well, this feller rode in on a big buckskin horse. Didn't say a word, just tied his horse and yanked off the riggin' and flung it over his shoulder and stamped into the harness-room. The puppy—I expect he figured it'd be old Bellingham—anyway, he waddled over waggin' his bony little tail and went right between this big feller's legs as he was swingin' the saddle to an empty rack. Dang near made the feller stumble . . . The feller stepped back and kicked as hard as he could. The pup went up against the wall with a squeal and fell in a heap with blood comin' from his mouth."

Walt said, "How do you know all this. Did you see it?"

"Not exactly. I was in the runway with Kelly. We heard the commotion and went over to the doorway. The feller had racked his saddle, saw us starin' at him, walked right by us like we wasn't even there, and went stampin' up out of the barn."

"Where was Bellingham?"

"Takin' the buckskin horse out back to a corral."

"Where is he now?"

"Last I seen, he was settin' in the harness-room with a hawgleg pistol."

"Either you or Kelly talk to him?"

Fred Tower raised his eyes. "Did you ever talk to a tree? His face was gray, and for once his hands wasn't shaky. He had put his puppy under some blankets with just his head stickin' out, like he was asleep . . . You know what Kelly said to me? 'You better go get Walt because sure as hell Bellingham's goin' after that feller and he'll get himself killed.' "

Walt looked for his hat, dropped it on the back of his head, and arose from the desk. "Where is this feller, Fred?"

He didn't know. "Maybe at the store or the saloon. I didn't watch which way he turned after he left the barn."

"What's he look like?"

"Big. About your size, maybe a little older, dark-looking. Bundled inside a sheep-pelt riding coat. Needs a shave. He's got a little button or something on the front of his hat." Fred Tower also stood up. "Want me to keep Bellingham out of it, Walt?"

"Think you can?"

"Yes. He's no match for a yaller dog—skinny, shakes, eyes run, and all. I can—if I got to—set on him."

"All right. I'll see if I can find this stranger."

Fred held the door, and as a gust of wind blew past them he said, "You be careful. He's not some drunk cowboy, Walt."

CHAPTER 2
Toward Day's End

THE clerk at the mercantile establishment shook his head at Walt. On windy days there wasn't so much trade he wouldn't have remembered a man who was big, dark, wearing a sheep-pelt coat with some kind of a little button on the front of his hat.

"Ain't been in here, Constable. Ain't been no strangers at all and precious few regular customers, weather bein' like it is and all. But it'll be hot again tomorrow."

Walt left and went to check the Horseshoe Saloon. Pat Flannery had just returned behind his bar from stoking the big stove and shook his head when Walt asked about the stranger. "No one like that, Walt. There was a couple of freighters earlier, and some cowmen—Gus Heinz among them, but no one like you described."

Constable Cutler returned to the roadway bound for the pool parlor. Over there the proprietor had not had a single customer since yesterday, nor had he seen anyone walk by out front who fit Walt's description.

Walt returned to the roadway, felt gusty wind begin to abate, and walked northward as far as the rooming house. Bertha was in her kitchen baking something that smelled tantalizingly of cinnamon. The room was hot, so Walt loosened his coat as he asked about a new roomer, a stranger; big and dark and with some kind of little button on the front of his hat.

Bertha Maloney dried both hands on an apron, filled two cups with hot coffee from the cookstove, put them both on the oilcloth-covered table, and pointed to a chair. She did not say a word until they were both seated.

She knew Walt Cutler as well as she knew anyone, and right now her interest was not in some big lummox of a cowman with a button on his hat. She had been thinking of Elizabeth Bartlett. Bertha had loaned the money so that Elizabeth could buy the Peralta Cafe, which was the only restaurant in town, but even if it hadn't been, Elizabeth's woman-cooked meals would have attracted male patrons the way sugar attracted flies. Not just because Elizabeth was an accomplished cook, either. She was also a handsome, full-bodied woman.

Since the death of Elizabeth's husband the previous year, Bertha had been like a mother hen, with Elizabeth as her only chick. She looked Walt Cutler squarely in the eye and said, "I want to talk to you about Elizabeth, Walt. It's not just the stockmen that are showing interest in her. There's plenty of men around town, including widower Jim McGregor. Good Lord, he's almost old enough to be her father. Him and the others . . ."

Walt relaxed in the warm kitchen studying the square-jawed female face across the table. "Put it in plain language," he told her.

Bertha sighed and rolled her eyes. Men! Strong as oak and twice as thick! "They're stumbling over each other trying to court her. It's enough to make a person want to chew nails and spit rust!"

Walt continued to gaze at the older woman. "Bertha, you told me to give her time."

Bertha Maloney nodded her head and dropped her gaze to the cup of black java in front of her. "Yes, I did. And I meant it. She's been improving for six, eight months, but she's still not all the way back yet."

"Well then, what can these rutting bucks accomplish?"

"Annoy her, upset her," exclaimed Bertha, eyes fiery. "They even come around her in the evenings wantin' her to go buggy-riding with them. Or for a walk."

"Does she go?"

"Of course not. They annoy her. She told me so."

Constable Cutler shifted, reached for his cup, and lifted it halfway as he said, "What do you want me to do?"

"Go stake your claim, Walt. Go over there right at supper time and let 'em see you got first claim."

Walt sipped coffee, put the cup down, and looked pained. "Bertha," he said in soft protest. "What can I do? Anyway, right there in front of a cafe full of people? You got any idea how I'd look, doing something like that?"

The rooming house proprietor was a naturally unyielding individual. "She thinks the world of you. You told me yourself you think the same of her. All right—then *you* take her buggy-riding. Let folks see the pair of you together. That'll thin them out, Walt. Keep them from pestering her. Widow-women are treated like this every blessed time. I know. When my Lester died years back I got the same attention."

Walt drank more coffee before looking quizzically at the older woman. "Widow-women? Why are they different from other single women, Bertha?"

She sat back, looking straight at him for a moment, said nothing but rolled her eyes again, and reached for the coffee cup.

Walt had an intuitive feeling that something had been settled, and it puzzled him. He slowly inclined his head. "All right. I'll take her buggy-riding."

Bertha put her cup down with more force than was necessary and her face showed exasperation. "Not just buggy-riding. Court her, Walt. It is time now. . . . Anyway, what is the name of this cowman with the button on his hat?"

"I don't know. He rode into town today. All I have is a description."

"Did you try Flannery's place?"

"Yes. And the general store, the pool hall, looked for him in the roadway, thought he might have taken a room up here."

"He hasn't. Is he an outlaw, Walt?"

"I don't know what he is, Bertha. I just want to find him, look him over, maybe talk to him a little."

Mrs. Maloney arose and motioned toward Walt's cup. "Care for more?"

He didn't, so he thanked her and went back down the creaky old dingy hallway to the porch out front, and while buttoning his coat, studied both sides of Main Street all the way to the lower end of town. There was no big, dark stranger on either plankwalk.

He struck out diagonally for the Horseshoe Saloon. Perhaps the stranger had reached the bar after Walt had left it. When Walt got there he was told the stranger had not been in, but Pat Flannery leaned his protruding gut against the bar and, in a conspiratorial tone of voice, informed Constable Cutler he had seen a man answering the description of the wanted stranger entering the cafe no more than fifteen minutes ago.

Walt left the saloon and was intercepted by Jim McGregor in front of the bank. McGregor was, as usual, attired in matching britches and coat, was wearing a white shirt and a necktie, looked every inch the progressive banker that he was, and had neatly trimmed his beard, which was iron gray. The banker was in one of his amiable moods as he said, "Thought you might be interested, Constable: the bank opened an account with a man named Ralph Warren this morning." McGregor paused for effect.

Walt glanced impatiently in the direction of the cafe, which was southward, on the opposite side of the road. McGregor caught hold of Walt's arm and leaned as though imparting a secret. "Ten thousand in cash to open the account."

Walt's attention was pulled away from the cafe. "Ten thousand dollars?"

McGregor beamed, hooked both thumbs in his vest pockets where a massive gold watch-chain dangled, and replied smugly, "Folks know about our bank a long ways off. We go after business. It's not like it was when old Alden White run things." McGregor leaned down a little as he said, "Mr. Warren's looking for investments. He represents four other moneymen. He told me that maybe they'd buy a stagecoach franchise and set up business here in Peralta."

Walt gazed at the large, beaming older man. "We already have a stagestop, Jim."

"Yes, but it's nothin' more'n a way station. What Mr. Warren is talking about would mean a big corralyard, hired hostlers, a thriving business, Walt, to bring money and outsiders to Peralta. It's what this town has been needing for—"

"Did he want to borrow money from the bank to start up, Jim?"

McGregor looked almost offended. "No. Certainly not. His ten thousand dollars is just to show us here in town that him and his partners are in good faith. That's all. He told me he's tied in with some of the biggest names in the investment business back East." McGregor suddenly stopped speaking and abruptly raised a thick arm. "There he is. That big feller in the rider's coat coming out of the cafe."

Walt stood like a statue watching the big, dark stranger button his coat, clear his pipes, and expectorate into the roadway. The constable was too distant to make out the details of the stranger's face but he did not have to be closer to recognize the expensive boots, coat, beaver-belly hat, and the hand-carved gunbelt and holster that showed slightly below the sheep-pelt coat on the right side.

He could not see the button on the man's hat so he asked McGregor if he had seen it. The banker had. "Little gold horseshoe. No bigger'n your little fingernail. For good luck, I guess. Why don't you go down there and introduce yourself? He asked if we had decent law enforcement in Peralta."

Walt nodded and started to cross the road. The big man he was watching did the same, leaving the rough boards in front of the cafe, then crossing directly toward the log jailhouse. Walt picked up his gait a little and recrossed the road. As Walt approached the jailhouse, the big man emerged from the empty office. They met near the doorway, and if first impressions were important, the one Walt Cutler had of Ralph Warren was of determination, for although the stranger smiled as he extended his hand and mentioned his name, it was the kind of an expression that meant he was measuring Constable Cutler against something inherent in himself.

Walt led the way inside and left the roadway door open because the wind had died and the heat was rising. He offered coffee, which Warren declined as he got comfortable in the same chair Fred Tower had last sat in.

Warren had black hair, dark eyes, and a tendency to swarthiness that had been augmented by exposure. He had a sprinkling of gray at the temples, was barrel-chested, and had a look of physical strength. His gaze was direct, almost challenging. He had a pair of black riding gloves folded over under the elaborately hand-carved shellbelt which were visible when he unbuttoned his sheep-pelt coat.

Walt guessed he was probably in his late forties or early fifties. The constable draped his hat and coat from buck antlers behind the desk and sat down as he said, "Usually this late in the season we don't get many strangers in Peralta. Unless they come in on the stage, maybe stay overnight, and head out in the morning."

It was a noncommittal thing to say. The big man accepted it that way and replied in a deep voice, "I expect that's true in a lot of towns. I'm here because my partners back East are interested in towns with futures. Most towns got some kind of opportunity. Your place needs a real stageline. Not just set up here but with headquarters here. What you got, Constable, don't amount to much more'n a way station."

Walt leaned on the desk listening and studying Ralph Warren, the investor who kicked puppies to death.

Warren smiled. "There's a big empty place south of the rooming house and north of the bank. Maybe an acre or two. It's the exact right location for a palisaded, big corralyard. Horse stalls along the back wall, a bunkhouse back there too for hostlers, drivers, gunguards away from home. And plenty of room along the main road for the office . . . Constable, I'm talking about a business that'd bring trade and give a lot of jobs." The black eyes were fixed on Walt. "Part of my interest is in the quality of law enforcement Peralta's got. If we get a mail franchise and maybe get set up for transporting bullion and all, we'd want to be plumb sure there is someone who could look out for us against outlaws."

Walt spoke dryly. "There are some men around town I call on now an' again as possemen. You can ask around about me, about my ability to maintain order and go after anyone who needs going after."

Ralph Warren listened, seemed satisfied, and made another remark about the proposed new stageline company. "We'd have our own gunguards. In fact a couple of them were supposed to meet me down at Gloria. Maybe they missed the train. Anyway, they weren't there so I saddled up and rode north by myself. They'll show up eventually. I got in mind riding the roads our stages will use, get the feel of the land, see what it's like and all."

Walt eyed the little golden horseshoe on the big man's hat. Warren saw the look, removed the hat, looked at the small horseshoe himself, and faintly smiled as he said, "It was given to me by a lady some years back. Because she said I was lucky."

Warren dropped the hat back atop his head. The subject of the little golden horseshoe was closed. Walt decided that Ralph Warren was one of those individuals who dominated and controlled conversations. Maybe other things as well. He was a man who would have opinions which were not subject to change or to argument. He was a very confident, probably very capable, strong-willed man, but not a flexible one, and if he got angry he would be very dangerous. It was not just the way he wore his Colt that inclined Walt toward this judgment; it was the way Warren spoke, the tone he used, the way he allowed no time for anyone else to speak until he wanted them to, the obvious sense of physical power the man had.

He asked if Walt knew who owned that piece of ground he had mentioned. Walt answered shortly. "A feller named Fred Tower owns it. He owns the saddle and harnessworks in town. He used to have a tannery on that ground, until the town council asked him to move it because folks objected to the smell and the flies."

Ralph Warren leaned to arise, his eyes on Walt. "I saw the harness shop. I'll go talk to Mr. Tower." He arose and started toward the door, but turned and said, "That lady who owns the cafe—is she single, do you know?"

"She's a widow, Mr. Warren. Her husband died last year."

The big man moved to the open door. "I never expected to see anyone like her in Peralta, Constable. It was nice to meet you."

Walt remained at his desk until the big, dark man was out of sight, then picked up his hat and crossed the road to the cafe. It was a tad early for dinner so the cafe was empty when he entered. Elizabeth raised green eyes, put aside the ragged newspaper she had been reading, smoothed her apron, and said, "Constable . . ."

He sat at the counter looking at her—and felt the back of his neck getting red, but he pressed ahead. "Hot days."

She nodded, "But beautiful evenings, Constable."

He could feel the relief sweep through him. He had not been able to think of the way to get that buggy-riding business into the conversation, but she had presented him with exactly what he needed. He said, "You're right, evenings are fine. But the days are gettin' shorter, so if folks was figurin' on buggy-riding they'd want to start early, wouldn't you say?"

She sat down on a stool behind the counter, gazing at him from eyes that seemed to be darkening through the period when she did not reply.

"Yes, I suppose they should start early, Constable."

He listened for encouragement and did not believe he had heard any. But then, he had not heard anything that had sounded like rejection either.

She started to arise from the stool as she said, "I'll get you some coffee."

"Wait," he exclaimed, and watched her slowly ease back atop the stool, large eyes looking steadily, and unnervingly, at him. "Yes, Constable?"

He looked slightly past her at the pie table where inverted platters prevented insects from reaching the pies and cakes. He sounded reproachful when he spoke again. "Elizabeth, last year we were down to first names. I still am." Calling him Constable all the time was not making this any easier.

She said, "Walt."

He continued to look slightly to one side as he said, "I'd be pleased if you'd go buggy-riding with me tomorrow night, Elizabeth . . . if you feel like it."

Her answer came so quietly, so naturally and easily, it flabbergasted him. "I'd be happy to. What time?"

He had not thought about the time. "Well, what time do you close up the cafe?"

"Seven . . . It'll be almost dark by then though, won't it?"

He nodded. He did not see darkness as an obstacle.

. She arose from the stool. "I'll close up at six," she announced and spoke over her shoulder as she was walking toward the cooking area. "I'll get your supper. There's an old newspaper you might want to look at."

He did not look at the newspaper, he looked at his hands, then over his shoulder to see if anyone was about to enter the cafe. No one was. He sat up straight and let go a long, audible sigh of relief.

CHAPTER 3
A Difficult Evening

WHEN Elizabeth brought his meal she smiled as she put it on the counter. "I haven't ridden in a real buggy since I was in my teens," she said.

He knew exactly what she meant. She had come to the Peralta country as the wife of a homesteader, riding in a large, heavy old wagon. Since then she'd faced one hardship after another until her husband's death the year before. He avoided showing sympathy; he'd shown her enough of that last summer. So had Bertha and a number of other people. Instead, he grinned and said, "O'Bryon's got a new top-buggy with yellow running gear. He has a weakness for good rigs and good horses."

She arose from the stool when a pair of unshaven freighters came in. They were rumpled, stained men, short on words and probably short on funds as well because when they asked Elizabeth what supper would cost, they dug deep and counted their silver coins before nodding at her.

She threw another smile at Walt as she moved past toward the kitchen, and he was halfway through his meal when Fred Tower walked in looking wilted and unhappy. He nodded toward the constable and sat down near him. He said, "Did I volunteer to mind old Bellingham or did you talk me into it?"

Walt grinned. "You volunteered. Why?"

"Well, he wouldn't give up his old gun, so while I stood in the harness-room doorway talkin' to him like a Dutch uncle, Kelly run up to Flannery's and got a bottle. We set it on the floor between us and him."

"And he took it?"

The harnessmaker nodded lugubriously. "Yes, he took it.

An' drunk two-thirds of it . . . He passed out. Walt, I wish you'd had to stand there with us an' watch that. Tears runnin' down his face, I guess half for the puppy an' half for himself for givin' in to that damned bottle. I haven't felt so miserable in a long while."

"Where's his old gun?"

"Kelly locked it in a box. . . . Did you find that man who killed his pup?"

Elizabeth brought Fred's supper and went down to feed the freighters. But Fred had no appetite. He shoved the platter aside and leaned both arms in its place.

Constable Cutler ate, drank coffee, and tried to figure a way to tell Tower that he had indeed found the stranger and had not done anything to him for killing the old man's dog. In the end, all he said was, "Yeah. I met him. He's some kind of moneyman, like Jim McGregor. He wants to build a big stage corralyard and all that goes along with it here in Peralta."

Fred turned his head. "And . . . ?"

"And—maybe get the mail franchise and haul bullion. . . . No, I didn't bring up the puppy, Fred."

"Why not, for Crissake?"

"Well . . . Another time."

Fred got up without another word and stalked out of the cafe. Elizabeth came along, looked at the untouched meal, at the tall, striding form crossing in the direction of the harnessworks, and seemed puzzled. "It's the same supper he usually has." She looked toward Walt. "Did he say why he didn't want it?"

"Not in so many words. He was down at the livery barn where that stringy old man who works for O'Bryon got drunk and passed out. It bothered him."

She took the untouched platter to her cooking area and did not return until several more diners came in, letting the door slam after them, then she appeared with her hair freshly brushed and shiny. As she passed Walt she said, "Six o'clock?"

He nodded as he was arising to count out silver coins. "Six o'clock," he replied, and saw the large-eyed looks he got as he was turning away from the counter. This was how Bertha had said he should act in front of other townsmen, but that had not been his intention. At the door he threw Elizabeth a smile and a wink, and she smiled back.

He made one round of the town, then returned to his desk at the jailhouse with some mail from the pigeonhole over at the general store.

As usual there were the perfunctory wanted dodgers mailed indiscriminately from as far east as Kansas and as far west as Oregon. He had never, to his knowledge, made an apprehension of a fugitive wanted in those distant places. His personal opinion was that outlaws did not seek strange territory after a killing or robbery but remained in country they knew well enough to hide in.

He filed the posters in a large wooden box with dozens of others like them and was sifting through some letters sent to the "Sheriff of Peralta, New Mexico Territory" by people who had lost a brother, a son, occasionally a husband, and whose letters were shots in the dark. Fred Tower walked in out of the early dusk looking grim and unfriendly. Walt leaned back, gesturing toward the chair Fred had used earlier. He did not say a word. The initiative belonged to the harnessmaker.

Fred sat and cleared his throat. They had been friends a long time, which meant a lot to most men, as it did to Fred, but he was still angry over the dead puppy and what his friend had had to say about it over at the cafe. But he had been struggling with himself, and now he said, "Well, I met the son of a bitch, too."

Walt got comfortable.

"It was about all I could do to keep from takin' the stove poker to him . . . He wants to buy that piece of land where the old tannery used to set."

Walt leaned down, opened a bottom drawer, and set a bottle of rye whiskey on the edge of the desk. Fred reached for it, took two swallows that made his Adam's apple bob like a cork, put the bottle back, and breathed deeply a couple of times before saying, "Thanks."

"Did you sell it to him?"

Fred turned an angry look toward the constable. "I wouldn't sell that man a fistful of ice if he was in hell settin' on all the money in the world. No! I told him it wasn't for sale."

Walt reached for the bottle and also swallowed a couple of times, then put the bottle back where his friend could reach it. "For what he says he wants, Fred, that's the only piece along Main Street that's big enough. Unless he went above town or south of town and set up his corralyard."

Fred disagreed. "There's a pretty fair-sized plot of ground over behind the bank. Bigger'n my piece. You know that ground—belongs to the bank."

Walt knew the ground. It was not on the main thorough-fare through town, which stage companies required; otherwise when they delivered passengers to a place, they had to walk through the town just to reach the main roadway. And there were other disadvantages, quite a number of them, in fact.

Walt sat back. "Maybe Warren will want it, an' for a damned fact Jim McGregor will sell it to him. Jim wants that stage company to set up here."

Fred pushed his lips out, was briefly silent, then sucked them back, and said, "Jim was right behind that big 'breed, or whatever he is. He come into the shop like someone had fired him out of a cannon. I told him flat out—no, I wouldn't sell that land to Mr. Warren. Jim got as red as a beet an' accused me of tryin' to ruin the town by holdin' back progress. He demanded to know why I wouldn't sell to Mr. Warren."

"What did you tell him?"

"I didn't. I just told him to get the hell out of the shop because I was real busy. And he left. But he was fit to be tied."

Walt watched Fred reach for the bottle, take two more

swallows, and replace it. For someone who had refused supper, the older man's lanky frame and steely eyes showed no signs of the liquor. Fred finally wagged his head. The old scarecrow down at O'Bryon's barn still haunted him. He cleared his throat again, which the constable knew from experience presaged something Fred had difficulty bringing up, and which Walt Cutler was almost certainly not going to approve of.

He was right. Fred fumbled through pockets for his Kentucky twist, squinted as he picked lint off it, bit off a cud, and offered the twist to Cutler, who refused. He'd tried that stuff once and thought he was going to die—wished to hell he would die, but he hadn't. Just looking at one of those twists now made him uncomfortable.

Fred arose, opened the roadway door, poked his head out to scan north and south, then pulled back and squirted amber almost as far as the middle of the road. He then resumed his seat and said, "Let me bring old Bellingham up here, Walt. You let him have one of the cells so's he'll be sleepin' up off the ground under real blankets. I'll undertake to get Miz Bartlett to fix up somethin' for breakfast and supper. . . . I'm here to tell you, that old man's sick and muddled-up, and he's slowly starvin' to death. I know what you're thinking. I've known him a long time, and that's true, but not until today did I have any notion how it must feel to be in his condition. . . . Any cell, Walt. I'll make him leave you alone and stay out of here down at the barn most of the day . . . Well?"

Walt arose to stride to the stove, tinkered with the damper, then methodically made a fresh pot of coffee under which he did not build a fire after putting the pot on the stove. Then he returned to the desk and dropped down. "The town council would have a fit," he said. "When folks found out old Bellingham was living here, they'd send around every other old gaffer."

Fred stood up and looked down his beaked nose. "In other words you won't do it? You're satisfied to let that sick, starvin' old rack of bones die down there some winter night when he takes the croup or something? Walt Cutler, I'll tell you what I saw when I was watching that old man. Me first, then you."

The constable got to his feet facing his friend. "Fred, this is a jail. You can see what would happen if I let Bellingham sleep here every night."

Fred was thinking. His expression was grim and antagonistic, but it was also faintly sly. He stormed out of the office the way he had done over at the cafe. But this time he strode southward, instead of northward in the direction of his harness shop.

Walt finally lighted the stove. He did not especially want any more coffee. He had drunk enough of the stuff today to float the ark. But someone might come along; they usually did of an evening, if for no other reason than to sit and talk. There were times when Constable Cutler could almost believe his jailhouse office was the clearing ground for all the gossip in the Peralta country.

An hour later as he was turning down the stove's damper, someone hurled the roadside door open so hard it went completely around and struck that chair Fred and the swarthy stranger had used. As Walt turned, the harnessmaker staggered inside, left the door open, and without even looking at the constable, yanked open the cell-room door with his left hand. He could not have used his right hand; it was holding tightly to an inert, whiskey-scented old bag of bones dressed like a scarecrow, who seemed to be weightless over Fred's shoulder.

Walt sprang to block him, too late. Fred marched down the dingy little corridor, entered one of the four strap-steel cages, eased his burden gently onto a wall bunk, pulled the folded army blanket at the foot of the cot up over old Bellingham, and turned defiantly as Constable Cutler filled the doorway, glaring.

"I want to sign a complaint against this here miscreant," he stormed, and shoved Walt aside as he stamped out of the cell. Walt looked at Fred with a dark scowl. "What do you think you're doing?"

"I'm delivering a criminal into your hands, Constable."

"Criminal? Fred, if you think you're goin' to get away with—"

"You just fill out the papers and I'll sign 'em, Mr. Cutler." Fred pointed a rigid finger at the unconscious old man on the wall bunk. "Thievery. He went and stole six leather halters, seven bridle headstalls, two sets of tapaderas and a set of silver conchos from my place of business. And I want to know when the circuit-ridin' judge is comin' to town."

Walt turned the harnessmaker with a powerful arm and herded him back to the office. He kicked the cell-room door closed after himself and pointed to a chair. "Sit down," he told the harnessmaker. "Fred! I said sit down! Now then—do I look like I came down in the last rain? That old skeleton in there couldn't have carried all that stuff you said he stole. But even if he could have carried it—he wouldn't have stolen it. Lots of people around town would have, maybe, but not old Bellingham. Ask O'Bryon how many times he's left Bellingham to run the barn and collect the money. Kelly told me that not once did he ever come up short when Bellingham was in charge.

"Fred, I know what you're trying to do. I knew it the minute you walked in carryin' him over your shoulder. . . . All right, he can stay here tonight. Just for tonight. Tomorrow you find him another place to stay."

"But he's sick, Walt. If you doubt me, go look for yourself. Or get Doc Eaton up here from Gloria to look at him."

Walt went to the open roadside door and jerked his head. "Go on home, and you better be here first thing in the morning to get Bellingham out of here, or so help me I'll kick him out and lock you up in the same cell. Now go on home!"

Walt closed the door after Fred Tower and stood glaring. "Doc Eaton," he growled. "He'd charge three dollars just to drive up here from Gloria. Twenty-two miles. An' what could he do after he got here? Nothing. Not a damned thing. When a man sets out to drink himself to death no doctor or anyone else can stop him. And that's a damned fact!"

CHAPTER 4
Another Day

FRED did not arrive the following morning after Constable Cutler had unlocked the jailhouse; Elizabeth Bartlett did, carrying two little tin pails, one half-full of hot stew that smelled delicious. The other small pail had fresh black coffee in it.

When Walt gazed stonily at her from behind his desk, she gave him that same heart-melting smile she had offered last evening at the cafe and said, "Have you taken him across the alley to the washhouse yet? I can wait if you haven't."

He put his hat atop the desk. She was watching him. When he looked up she glanced in the direction of the big, oaken cell-room door. "Maybe you could give him these pails, Walt. I really should be getting back. The breakfast trade will start filling up my counter soon." She put the pails on a wall bench and turned toward the door. Over there she turned to say, "Did the cat get your tongue?" Then she was gone.

He glared at the closed roadway door. "Cat! What cat? Fred's behind this. That old screwt went over to the cafe last night sure as hell and cried big crocodile tears to her. That conniving old sidewinder."

He got the pails, unlocked the cell-room door, and took them down to Bellingham's cell. The old man was awake, sweating, shaking, dabbing at his wet eyes as Walt let himself into the cell, pulled over a small stool, and put the pails on it. The constable said, "Sit up and—"

"I can't, Mr. Cutler. I tried. I just can't hoist myself." Bellingham wrinkled his nose and rolled his eyes around to the little pails. "Is that hot food? Constable, get a bucket will you, I'm goin' to be sick. I can't stand that smell."

Walt was undecided. In the end he hastened back to the office for a bucket and returned to place it beside the old man on the wall bunk.

Bellingham was not sick but he gulped a lot of air and rolled his eyes. Walt returned once more to the office and when he reentered the cell he stopped beside the bunk, slid an oaken arm beneath Bellingham's shoulders, and jack-knifed the old man into a sitting position, then handed him the whiskey bottle.

Bellingham would have drained it but Walt pulled it away after the old man had swallowed three times. Then he got the old man squared around on the cot in a sitting position, pushed the stool close, and removed the lid from the smallest pail first. "Black coffee," he announced, holding the pail up. "Drink it."

Bellingham's eyes were overflowing. He pushed a filthy old ragged cuff across his face in irritation.

Walt said it again. "Drink it!"

The old man struck petulantly at the pail and missed it by six inches. Walt's arm hardened behind Bellingham. "Pardner, you're going to drink this if I got to set on you and pour it down your gullet. *Drink it!*"

Bellingham drank, had a coughing fit, drank more, and gagged. Walt put the pail down and reached for the bucket, but nothing happened. He put the bucket aside and removed his supporting arm. Bellingham did not collapse. His bleary gaze wandered aimlessly and returned to Walt's face. "I feel like hell," he moaned. Walt had no trouble believing him. He also looked like hell. At one time Bellingham had been as large as Walt. Now, he probably did not weigh a hundred and twenty pounds. Bones showed through, his gut was shrunken, his color was faintly blue, and while either the whiskey or the coffee had steadied his hands, his eyes still ran tears.

He was not the first drunk Walt had had in his cells but the others he had known only casually if at all. Bellingham had been part of Peralta for a number of years. Like the town idiot, Bellingham was someone people glanced away from and avoided. In this small strap-steel cage there was no way to avoid looking at him.

Walt uncovered the second pail. Bellingham began gesturing with both arms. "No. Constable I can't do that. I'll heave it all over your cell."

Walt pulled the stool close to the bunk, grimly sat on it, and held up the pail. "Hot beef stew," he said, and looked into the pail. "With vegetables: carrots and potatoes and—"

Bellingham made a deep sound of distress and said, "The bucket! Give me the bucket!"

Walt moved quickly, but nothing happened this time either, except some noisy gagging. As Walt took back the bucket he eyed the old man. In a quiet voice he said, "You can't just guzzle whiskey, Bellingham. You got to eat."

"Why? Tell me why, Constable?"

"Well because—look at yourself. You're down to skin and bones, you got the shakes, your nose is running. Listen to me—just part of the stew."

"I can't. Constable, for Gawd's sake, I just plain can't." Bellingham's wet, pale eyes fixed themselves on Walt. "They took my pistol."

"I know they did."

"You let them take my gun? Do you know what the man did to my little puppy?"

Bellingham's eyes were brightening, his voice was steadying, he even fisted his hands. Walt let go a rattling sigh and raised the little pail. "Listen to me. Now pay attention. Yes, I know about your puppy and I know who killed it. . . . Now you eat at least half of this stew and—we'll talk about that son of a bitch."

The old man's gaze dropped fleetingly to the bucket, then fled. "I'm not hungry," he said. "Constable, I just don't have any appetite."

"Make yourself eat it. Mr. Bellingham, make yourself—"

"Mr. Bellingham? How come you to say that? No one's called me mister in ten years."

Walt pushed the pail closer. "Sure they have. Eat some of this."

Bellingham took the pail and held it in his lap. "No, they haven't, Constable. They don't even look at me. Little boys set their dogs on me; women cross the road rather than pass me on the plankwalks."

The old man's limpness had disappeared. He was sitting erect in his anger. "Old Bellingham who dungs out O'Bry-on's barn and crawls into his bottle every night. Old . . . Constable?"

"Yes."

Bellingham's nostrils fluttered, his wet eyes were briefly clear. "Constable, do you know my first name?"

Walt did not know it, had never heard it, or if he had, had not remembered it. He said, "John?"

"No! You didn't know it. No one does. Old Bellingham . . . Constable, I was a colonel in the Confederate army. A surgeon. I—Gawd!—you never saw so much blood and agony. I worked many a time twenty-four hours without stopping, except if someone offered me a bottle. Amputations . . . hunting knives and meat saws. Gangrene, stench, sawdust on the floors to sop up the blood . . . Four years, lacking four days. Colonel Death. That was my name for myself. Colonel Franklin Bellingham, Army of the Confederacy Medical Corps. Colonel Death."

Bellingham raised the pail and drank deeply of the stew, paused to chew and glare at Walt, then drank more and chewed more. He finished half the contents of the pail and handed it back as he said, "Do you have nightmares, Constable?"

"Now and then."

"I've had them every night and even sometimes in broad daylight for almost twenty years. They came to my table panting like dogs, sweat running off them like water, blue in the face, their eyes dilated from the laudanum. And I killed them. Saw the leg off, drop it on the floor while orderlies sear the stump with hot pokers. Or the arm. Or I'd dig up to my wrists in their slippery guts for lead. . . ." Bellingham looked longingly at the bottle in Walt's pocket. "And gangrene."

Walt arose briskly, picked up the two little pails, and closed the cell door after himself. He was afraid that if he remained a minute longer he would hand over the bottle. From the corridor he said, "I'll be back directly to take you across the alley to the washhouse . . . Bellingham? Frank—maybe you should have done this more often."

"Done what—eat stew?"

"You know what I'm talkin' about. Get it out of your system; spit it out, yell it out if you want to, cuss it out, but do it. . . . I'll be back directly."

Cutler closed the cell-room door with his foot and put the pails on the edge of his desk, returned the whiskey bottle to its place in a bottom drawer, and went over to open the roadway door and stand in the opening, taking down deep sweeps of fresh morning air with a chilly taste to it.

Across the road the general store was open for business, and nearby the cafe had steamy windows and a stream of men coming and going. Northward, Flannery was flinging his scrub-water into the roadway, and Gus Heinz was coming south in his old ranch wagon for supplies. He had one of his tall, broad-shouldered sons with him. According to saloon gossip, Gus was about ready to start his twenty-two-mile cattle drive down to the shipping pens at Gloria. Walt watched the wagon angle close to the plankwalk over in front of the general store and thought the saloon talk was probably accurate if Heinz was in town today to load up supplies.

Gus was not a man who would drive from his ranch in the northeasterly foothills to Peralta without a damned good reason. He was a short, gruff, pale-eyed man built like a bear, and occasionally displayed a similar disposition. Heinz was one of those no-nonsense, hard-working, frugal cattlemen whose one weakness was poker.

Walt's attention moved southward, where the northbound stage from Gloria was slackening to a rattling walk at the edge of town. Peralta had an ordinance against large rigs passing through town at any gait faster than a walk. He knew the driver, a bearded old ruffian named Mack Bennett who would fight at the drop of a hat, occasionally drank too much, and who could tool either a four-horse hitch or a six-horse hitch on a strung-out curve to pass through a place where a small top-buggy would have had difficulty.

As the rig passed, Bennett saw Walt in his doorway, grinned through his beard, and waved. Walt grinned and waved back. He had dragged Mack by the scruff of his neck from the Horseshoe to his jailhouse many times, locked him up until he was sober, then turned him loose. Once, Mack had called him. Just once. Mack never tried that again. They were friends. Each of them respected what they recognized as the particular talent of the other.

There were two hard-faced men inside Mack's coach. They too eyed Constable Cutler as the rig moved past. But they did not smile.

That big, dark man with the little gold horseshoe on his hat emerged from the cafe and stood at the edge of the plankwalk as the stage went slowly past. He lighted a cigar, his black eyes fixed on the two men inside, and when he had a good head of fragrant smoke rising, he stepped down into the roadway to cross over and walk in the direction of the way station.

Walt returned inside, got Bellingham out of the cell, and herded him across the alley to the washhouse. He usually used leg-irons on prisoners for this trip but Bellingham was not really a prisoner.

He showed the old man where the jailhouse razor and soap were and grinned as Bellingham looked troubled. Ever since Walt had known the old man, he had either not shaved, or his face looked like he'd been clawed by cats. "Take your time," he said. Then he stood aside and waited.

Bellingham did a creditable job with the old straight razor, looked critically at himself in the steel mirror, and turned. "That razor wouldn't cut hot butter," he grumbled.

Walt laughed. "Maybe not. But you didn't cut yourself. . . . Let's go back now."

Bellingham stood fast. "Wait. I'm not a prisoner, am I?"

"Not exactly, no."

"Then I'll just walk on down the alley to the barn and get to work."

Walt put his head slightly to one side. "Frank—what's buried under the old horse-blankets in the harness-room down there? Naw, you come on back with me. At least for a while."

Bellingham stamped through the jailhouse storeroom to the office and squared around on Walt with fire in his eyes. "If I'm not a prisoner, then what right have you got . . . ?"

Walt had moved around behind the desk. He leaned down to open the lowest drawer and straightened up to put the whiskey bottle on the desk. He did not say a word, just watched the older man and waited.

Bellingham grabbed the bottle and swallowed rapidly. Walt took it away from him and pointed to the cell-room. "Frank, you just lie down now for an hour or so."

The old man waited until he had been locked in and the constable was gone, then went to his bunk, stretched out full length, and closed his eyes.

Walt raised the bottle for a critical examination, then was putting it back into the drawer when the saddle- and harnessmaker walked in with a springy step and a warm and handsome smile.

Walt did not smile back. "You were supposed to come around here a couple of hours ago and get him out of here, Fred."

The harnessmaker went to his favorite chair, sat down, and said, "An' a good morning to you too, Constable."

Walt noticed a stalk of dead grass on his trousers, probably picked up across the alley. He flicked it off, followed its flight, and went over to search for coals in the stove. There were none, so he fed in a wad of paper, two handfuls of dry kindling, dropped in the match, and closed the curved iron door. The coffee would be hot in a while. He went over to perch on a corner of the desk and eye his visitor. "Fred—what's Bellingham's first name?"

He blinked. "First name? Bellingham, that's all I ever heard. Why?"

"It is Franklin."

Fred was studying Constable Cutler through a pair of puzzled eyes. "Franklin. Well, now, I'd say that was a nice name, wouldn't you?"

"You conniving old goat. You went over to Elizabeth last night and talked her into feeding him, didn't you?"

"I never did no such a damned thing. I paid her cash on the barrelhead to feed him. I never talked her into anything. . . . We had a little palaver. Just general talk is all. She knew who he was." Fred arose looking uncomfortable. "Well, I got to cut some skirts and jockeys today an' get 'em onto a saddle for Gus Heinz. Sure as hell he'll be comin' after them by noon. . . . Why is it that men who been on saddles all their blessed lives think a feller can make them like new after twenty years of neglect, an' do it in a couple of hours? Nice talkin' to you, Walt."

CHAPTER 5
Angry Men

KELLY O'Bryon appeared at the jailhouse looking for his dayman. Walt pointed to the chair against the front wall and said, "Sit down, Kelly. I got a couple of questions to ask you."

O'Bryon sat, hitched at his paunch to get comfortable, then eyed the constable while vigorously scratching his head. He said, "Walt, if he's done something . . . I'll pay the damage. Within reason, you understand."

Walt perched on the corner of the desk. "How much do you pay old Bellingham?"

O'Bryon stopped scratching, dropped his hat back down, and looked from Constable Cutler to the toes of his badly overrun boots. "Enough," he said softly.

"How much is enough, Kelly?"

"Well . . . he drinks it up about as fast as I give it to him."

"One last time, Kelly: how much?!"

"It works sort of like this. I give him a place to sleep, sort of look after him, take him to the cafe with me now and then, an' when he's shakin' I give him enough to go up to the Horseshoe and get his nerves settled."

Walt arose from his perch and went behind the desk, which was actually a very large table with drawers. He considered his clasped hands. He was not going to get a correct answer. He heard O'Bryon shifting in the chair and raised his eyes. "I think you better hire another dayman," he said.

O'Bryon reacted as though he had been stung. "What! . . . What did he do? You're goin' to keep him locked up? Listen, Constable, I don't know where to go to find someone to replace him with."

Walt smiled. "You can find someone. But next time you might have to pay a wage."

O'Bryon got red. "Bellingham gets every bit he's worth. About half the time he can't hold his hands still, or he's sick, or he's passed out in the harness-room."

Walt nodded. He and Kelly O'Bryon were old friends, exactly as he and Fred Tower were old friends. But as far as Walt was concerned, neither man was packing around an overwhelming burden of virtue. Walt said, "What's old Bellingham's first name?"

O'Bryon blinked. "Franklin. He told me that one time when he was smoked to the gills. Said he'd been an army surgeon. Whiskey-talk . . . About that little puppy—"

The constable arose. "Never mind, Kelly. Bellingham stays in a cell."

"What did he do, Walt?"

"Drunk and troublesome—for openers."

"Well, what the hell; that's only a day or two, until a man sobers up."

Walt shrugged powerful shoulders. "Get someone to take his place for a while. As for paying expenses—"

O'Bryon was out of his chair halfway to the door as he said, "All right. He's your prisoner. The law's got to be obeyed. I know that." He did not hesitate even long enough to close the door after himself.

Walt was turning back toward the desk when three large men blocked out roadway sunlight as they came into the jailhouse office. Cutler recognized Ralph Warren and nodded. He had seen Warren's companions earlier. They had been the unsmiling passengers in the morning stage up out of Gloria.

Warren introduced them. The man with the closely spaced hazel eyes was Herman Smith. The other man, who had a thin, long scar under his left ear that angled around toward his chin but did not reach quite that far, was named Buck

Jensen. He looked to be perhaps ten years younger than Herman Smith, who was beginning to gray a little.

After Cutler had arisen to shake hands, Warren explained that these men were the gunguards he had been waiting for. He said they were on their way down to O'Bryon's barn to rent three horses and explore the stage routes around the Peralta country.

The younger man smiled at Constable Cutler. "I heard about you down at Gloria," he said. "Had a little touch of the cramps and went to the doctor down there. Feller named Eaton. He said he knew you."

Walt made a small smile. He and Doctor Eaton had never been close and never would be. "Did he fix your bellyache, Mr. Jensen?"

"Well, yes. He gave me a big enough dose of salts to unplug an elephant."

Warren laughed easily. "Constable," he murmured, nodded, and led his companions back out to the roadway.

Walt went down the dingy little cell-room corridor. Frank Bellingham was sleeping—and sweating. It wasn't really that warm outside; it was even cooler inside the thick-walled jailhouse. Walt went in, gently covered the old man, tiptoed back out, locked the cell door, and returned to his office.

The day was half spent. He made a round of the town, nodded to people he knew, and heard loud voices at the harnessworks, so he crossed over and walked into the middle of an argument between Fred Tower and red-faced, bull-necked Gus Heinz. At sight of Walt, Fred waved his arms and said, "I told you! They throw saddles on the ground, leave 'em in the rain, let summer heat curl the leather, then they come in here and expect me to make 'em like new in—"

"New!" exclaimed the red-faced stockman. "Constable, I walked in here to ask how the work was goin' and this old goat landed right in the middle of me. No reason, except that maybe he's got something troublin' him. That bad knee he got last year—or maybe he tried to spark that lady at the cafe an' she bit his ear off, the darned old scalawag."

Fred started from behind his counter, head down and scarred hands curled into fists. Walt moved swiftly between them and met Fred with a glare. "Get back behind there," he said evenly.

Heinz had not yielded an inch. "Let him come. Get out'n the way, Constable."

Walt acted as though he had not heard the cowman. "Fred, you get back behind that counter, or I'll drag you down and put you in the same cell with your friend, and you can clean up the place where he heaved all over the floor. *Get!*"

This time Fred obeyed, but with the counter between them again he glared at Gus Heinz. "You knew you'd need this saddle a month ago. But no, you had to wait until the last damned day. Well—for all I care you can make your darned drive ridin' bareback like a squaw Indian! Now get out of here; I got work to do."

Walt escorted the angry cowman from the store and across the road to the Horseshoe. Pat Flannery set up two thick glasses of sudsy brown beer, collected his coin from Walt, and went up the bar where he'd been reading a newspaper. The saloon was empty except for the three of them. Walt raised his glass. "Here's to a good drive, Gus."

The shorter man nodded bleakly and drank deeply, then put his glass down and looked quizzically at the constable. "I give you the plain truth, Walt. I walked in an' barely got my mouth open and he lit on me with all four feet. . . . Is somethin' really wrong; is he ailin' or something?"

Walt considered his glass. "Was there anyone else around when you went in, Gus?"

"No. Not when I walked in. But just before I got over there three men were leavin' the shop. One of 'em had a little gee-gaw on the front of his hat. Strangers to me."

Walt raised his glass and drained it. He gave Heinz a rough slap on the shoulders. "I'll go talk to him. Maybe he'll settle down."

"Constable, before you go—I sure would like to have that saddle today before we leave town."

Walt smiled from the doorway. "I'll see what I can do."

Fred was rolling moistened leather in burlap to soften it up before it was worked when Cutler returned. He looked up, glared, then went back to work. Walt leaned on the counter. "What did Ralph Warren want, Fred?"

"Well, it started out with him repeating what he said yestiddy. About that piece of land where my tannery was, but when I turned him down again—he had a couple of other fellers with him—when I said it wasn't for sale at no price, one of these other fellers leaned over the counter, looked mean at me, and said that fellers who get in the way of progress sometimes turn up in graveyards."

Walt's interest quickened. "What did he look like?"

"Maybe a little shorter'n I am, had eyes real close to the bridge of his nose. Sort of tan-lookin' eyes. Walt, I'll tell you for a fact I've been judgin' folks for seventy years, and that feller's mean all the way through." Fred paused to look at the constable with less hostility in his gaze. "After they left, Gus Heinz walked in . . . I was thinkin' that from now on I'm goin' to put my six-shooter on the shelf under the counter, an' the next man that walks in here lookin' for trouble is goin' to get it."

Walt let his gaze wander among the racks of saddles, most of them showing new skirts, stirrup-leathers, fenders, seating-leathers or repaired saddlehorns. Eventually he said, "Gus came in at a bad time."

Fred grudgingly agreed. "I expect he did. It didn't help none that I'd just finished cuttin' leather for his darned saddle when he asked if it'd be ready in an hour or such a matter." He met the constable's gaze, then shifted stance so he would not have to do this, and mumbled. "Is he still in town?"

"Yeah. Over at the Horseshoe."

Fred pointed to a hand-carved A-fork saddle with rounded skirts and sterling conchos. "If you see him again tell him I'll loan him that Visalia saddle. They don't come any better." The harnessmaker faced around again looking ashamed. "That ought to be as good as apologizin', wouldn't you say?"

Walt kept his face solemn. "I'd say so. I'll tell him. Fred, when Mr. Warren came in with those two strangers, did he introduce you to them?"

"Nope. Didn't even act like they was with him. He got right off on the subject of me peddlin' him that land. Them two fellers stood aside listening and sayin' nothing until that weasel-eyed one got into it. . . . Walt, you know who he is?"

"Warren told me the two are gunguards for his stage company."

Fred turned that over in his mind, then gently wagged his head. "If that weasel-eyed one is a gunguard, Gawd help any poor deluded idiot who even looks like he's goin' to stop a stage that man is riding on."

Walt returned to the roadway, saw Gus and his son talking in front of the Horseshoe, and ambled over there to explain about the Visalia saddle. Gus looked at Walt from testy, pale eyes. He was on the verge of making an unkind remark, but Walt headed that off. "You stay here. Let your boy go get the saddle."

Heinz did not argue, and the wide-shouldered young Heinz headed for the harnessworks.

Gus watched him, then shrugged gorilla-like shoulders and appeared willing to forget the unpleasantness. As he told the constable, he had a wagon loaded with supplies, a big gather at the homeplace to be bedded down tonight, and a lot of penny-ante details to take care of before first light tomorrow, all of it much more critical to him than anything that had transpired between himself and Fred Tower. But he clung to the idea that perhaps Fred was ailing.

"Maybe if he'd go down to Gloria and see Doc Eaton. Worms, most likely, or too much whiskey." Heinz smiled and shoved out his hand. Walt pumped it, wished him well on the drive, and headed for the jailhouse. By now Frank Bellingham should be awake, and if he was, Walt had in mind getting more food down him. Maybe a couple more swallows of whiskey too, but less of that as time went on.

He was in front of the cafe preparing to cross over when a soft voice said, "Six o'clock."

He turned, saw the twinkle in her eyes from the doorway, and smiled. "Six o'clock."

"I'll bring along a picnic hamper, Walt."

He stopped. "Elizabeth, I got to tell you something."

"You don't like picnic food?"

"No. I am real fond of picnic grub. I was goin' to say you're prettier than a speckled pony. . . . Six o'clock. Oh—I almost forgot. Could I get a pail of grub for old—for Frank Bellingham?"

"When do you want it?"

"Any time. I'll go see if he's awake, then be right back over for it."

She laughed at him. "Any time."

He crossed the road with a spring in his step. It occurred to him that he should have talked to Kelly O'Bryon earlier in the day to be sure he could get the new rig with the yellow running gear. Now he would have to feed Frank first, and by then maybe someone else would have spoken for the buggy.

He would just have to take a chance on that.

Bellingham was not only awake, he was very thirsty, so Walt took a canteen of water down to him. Bellingham tipped his head and noisily drank. As he was handing the canteen back through the straps he said, "How come you don't have a coffee can in these cells? All afternoon I've had to pee so bad my back teeth are floating—and somethin' else, Constable . . ."

Walt slowly wagged his head. "I'll get the coffee can, then I'll fetch your supper. An' maybe, just maybe, after you've eaten, I'll fetch you a dram of—medicine."

CHAPTER 6
Toward Dusk

OVER at the cafe early diners were noisily eating all along the counter. Jim McGregor was among them, a handkerchief tucked inside his collar and arranged to protect his vest. He nodded to the constable and continued with his meal, but when Walt went to the upper end of the counter where Elizabeth had two pails, the moneyman's small, bright eyes missed nothing that passed between the woman and the lawman. Nor did many of the other diners, even though they did not appear to be watching.

Walt leaned and said, "I'll get a rig right after I've fed Bellingham," and she smiled as he was turning away. That did not escape a number of watching eyes either.

The heat was leaving; there seemed to be a faint skiff of cloudiness, like a veil, between the setting sun and the earth below. It was going to be a cool, beautiful night for buggy riding.

Frank Bellingham had just finished lustily blowing his nose when Walt unlocked the cell and entered with the little pails. Bellingham eyed them. There had been changes in him, not spectacular changes, but definite ones. Walt's first inkling of this was when Frank kept gazing at the pails Walt was putting on the small stool as he said, "Make a trade with you, Constable. I'll eat the stew and drink the coffee, if you'll fetch the bottle down here so's I can have a jolt first."

There had not been a single pause, nor a moment of the kind of mildly confused hesitation that usually intervened between something Bellingham started out to say and finally finished saying.

Walt straightened up from the stool, looking steadily at the old scarecrow. He wanted to grin. "Eat first," he told the older man. "Get something down there to take up the slack when the jolt comes along." He went to the cell door, stepped beyond it, and turned back. They regarded one another in silence, then Cutler went after the bottle.

In the office he tossed his hat atop the desk, got the bottle, and wagged his head. He was beginning to enjoy this. Not for any particular reason that he could define; simply because it made him feel good to think that he just darned well might succeed in helping old Bellingham get back some self-respect.

Fred Tower poked his head in from out front. "Y'know what? Gus drove his wagon over in front of the shop on his way out of town and yelled for me to come out. When I did, he never said a damned word, he just handed me one of them two-bit cigars Flannery imports from back East. Then he whistled up his hitch and drove off with his back as straight as a ramrod."

Walt laughed. "Good. For someone like Gus that was a hard thing to do, and Fred—it wasn't him that should have apologized. You know that, don't you?"

"Yes . . . What are you doin' with that bottle? You takin' to drinkin' in private?"

Walt's eyes stopped smiling. "No, you conniving old goat. I'm rationing it out to Frank Bellingham, and that's your fault too."

Fred continued to eye the bottle from an expressionless face as he laconically said, "I'd never have figured you to be the type for breast-feeding." He slammed the door and ran.

Walt returned to the cell. Both pails were empty, and Bellingham was standing so close to the door Walt had to push him back to enter. Bellingham reached for the bottle. Walt let him have it, counted three swallows, and took the bottle back. For a fact, the old Secesh surgeon's mind was clearing a little. He was getting as sly as a weasel. Each of those three swallows had been taken after he had filled both his gullet and his mouth with whiskey. He had taken on about twice the load Walt had permitted him earlier.

Bellingham's eyes sprang water. He dashed a filthy sleeve over his upper face and panted like a dog as he said, "That is powerful whiskey, Constable, but it's got taste. . . . I got to sit down."

Walt retrieved the pails, locked the cell, and returned to the office to stow the bottle, which was almost empty now. Then he dropped on his hat and crossed over to the cafe. There was a Closed sign in the window next to the door but the counter still had four diners. Jim McGregor was among them. He was finishing his supper with a wedge of dark cake big enough to choke a horse. He winked at Walt and scraped his plate for the last crumb, then arose, tugging loose his handkerchief, spilled coins atop the counter, and jerked his head for Walt to follow him outside.

The banker produced a toothpick and used it with an experienced hand as he spoke while looking up and down the roadway. "I don't think I'm supposed to tell you this, Walt. It wasn't definitely said that I shouldn't. It was said, though, that what I'm goin' to tell you is a secret, and we'd ought to make damned sure it remained that way."

"Tell me what?"

McGregor flung the toothpick away and faced Cutler with a set of narrowed eyes. "Mr. Warren's already gettin' things organized. I tell you, that man's the best thing that's happened to Peralta since—I don't know when."

The constable said, "Fred don't think so."

McGregor made an exasperated gesture. "Fred! That darned old reactionary . . . But he's goin' to sell Mr. Warren that piece of ground. So help me, he is. Walt, damned if I'll let this opportunity slip away from us. He told me this evening that he might have to go find another town if Fred don't let him have that ground for his buildings and all. We can't let that happen. You'n Fred are real close friends. I want you to talk sense to him. He'd listen to you, maybe even to Pat Flannery or Kelly O'Bryon before he'd listen to me. Constable, he's got to sell Mr. Warren that piece of land. It's no earthly good to him any more, not since he got out of the tannery business. . . . Mr. Warren told me he thinks Fred won't sell to him because for some damned reason Fred don't like Mr. Warren."

Walt fidgeted; the last diners had been shooed out of the cafe. Elizabeth was closing up for the night. He said, "Jim . . . I'll come up to the bank in the morning an' we can talk some more."

"Wait," exclaimed the banker, and leaned closer, eyes narrowed again. "What I was goin' to tell you: like I said, Mr. Warren's already gettin' things organized." McGregor paused, then lowered his voice when he continued speaking. "There's a big mine south of Gloria called the Double Eagle. They sell bullion bars to the Denver mint. Been doin' that for years. They haul the bullion up to Gloria an' send it round-about up to Denver. Been doin' it like that for years too."

Walt nodded impatiently. He knew about the mine and those shipments. Everyone did. "Jim—"

"Let me finish . . . Mr. Warren knows some high officials at the Double Eagle. He's talked them into cuttin' the distance damned near in half by using his company. They'll pick up the bullion at Gloria, fetch it up to Peralta, transfer it to war wagons—you know what war wagons are: big freight outfits with double oak sides, loopholes for gunguards down inside and—"

"Jim, I know what war wagons are."

"Well . . . his company'll send those wagons beeline straight overland to Denver with way stations on the route and gunguards all along the way. . . . You see what I'm gettin' at? Ralph Warren's a real businessman. We got to get that piece of land for him. He's goin' to revolutionize this damned cow-town, Walt."

Walt heard a door open and turned. Elizabeth was looking at him. He said, "Jim . . . in the morning," and walked away.

McGregor watched Elizabeth hand a wicker hamper to the constable and cross the road beside him on their way down to O'Bryon's barn. He grunted to himself, annoyed, and went in the direction of Flannery's saloon.

Light was failing. Kelly O'Bryon was balancing on a rickety chair to light the two carriage lamps which outlined the doorless front opening of his place of business. He twisted at the sound of footfalls, saw Walt and Elizabeth Bartlett, and nearly lost his balance as he climbed down from the old chair. He knew what a picnic hamper was.

He smiled broadly. "Rig?" he asked. Walt's answer was brief. "The new one, Kelly. The one with yellow running gear—if it's here."

O'Bryon hitched at his britches; one of the difficulties men who had paunches encountered was that they tended to push a man's britches down. "It's here," he said, leaving the chair where it stood to lead the way down his earthen runway. "I got it parked across the alley in my wagon shed." He led the way through yellow lampglow from two hanging lanterns in the runway, halted in the alley, and looked at Elizabeth as he pointed to the new buggy. "You ever see anything that pretty?" He did not await her reply but went over to lift the shafts as though to pull the rig out of its sheltered place. "Look there; y'know, I been buyin' an' sellin' rigs for forty years an' this here is the first one I ever saw that had cherubs painted on the sideboards up front below the seat. Ain't they something to look at? Whoever painted them was real good at his trade. . . . Walt, lend me a hand. We'll pull it up inside. I been usin' that big Morgan mare with it. Daisy. Big Daisy. She's as good as gold, gentle as a lamb, don't shy. . . . Pull, Walt."

Inside, where the light was marginally better, Kelly ran his hand over the leather upholstery, which was red, handled the whip in its socket, pointed out the rolled-up side flaps with their genuine isinglass windows, and when Walt impatiently asked where the Morgan mare was, Kelly looked reproachfully at him and ignored Walt to address Elizabeth. "Now then, ma'am, wouldn't you think folks here in town'd help one another?"

Elizabeth nodded.

With that much encouragement Kelly hitched up his britches and faced Walt. "I can't do all the work around here, like cleaning this here buggy and everything else, all by myself."

Walt reddened. "I told you: hire another dayman."

Kelly flung his arms wide. "Where? I asked around. Usually Flannery knows if there's someone in town needs work. He told me flat out there wasn't anybody. . . . Walt, how about him sleepin' at the jailhouse and comin' to work durin' the day?"

Walt glared. "Where is the Morgan mare, Kelly?!"

O'Bryon gave up, flapped his arms against his sides, rolled his eyes, and went grumbling down among the stalls. Elizabeth said, "Are you being hard on him?"

Walt fumed in silence. As Kelly was walking back leading a twelve-hundred pound, stud-necked seal-brown mare, he answered her. "Elizabeth, it's partly because of him old Bellingham is like he is. We can talk about it later."

Not a word was said as Walt and Kelly backed the mare between the shafts and cooperated in harnessing her. She was indeed a perfectly mannered, friendly, and docile big animal. Walt put the hamper in back, handed Elizabeth up, went around to even up the lines as he climbed in, and turned to look at O'Bryon, still without a word passing between them. He talked up the mare and turned northward up the darkening roadway. There were a few pedestrians, mostly townsmen or rangemen loafing in front of the Horseshoe or over at the pool hall. The warmth was greater than it had been lately at night, but this time of year there was only one certainty: the nights would get coldest before dawn.

Where he left the road a mile north, it was to turn eastward. The land was more attractive west of the road, but that was the direction of the burned-out Bartlett homestead. He did not want any memories to trouble her. The agonies she had suffered were only a year old. They wouldn't be hard to resurrect.

They had gently rolling country to traverse. She studied his profile and wisely remained silent until the clenched jaw loosened and he turned to smile. Then she said, "People know you have old Bellingham in a cell. Mr. McGregor told me he'd heard that you are trying to dry him out. He said he didn't believe that was a constable's responsibility."

Walt leaned back with slack lines. Big Daisy was heading in roughly the correct direction. Maybe she'd been over to the little sweetwater spring in its bosque of shaggy old trees before. He said, "Elizabeth, you ever notice that in this world most people got tongues that hinge in the middle and flap at both ends?"

She laughed. "Yes, I suppose so."

"Well, McGregor's an aggressive businessman, and I suppose that's good. Lord knows old man White who ran the bank before sure wasn't. He blocked every new store and business and hardly ever approved of a loan except to stockmen. But Jim's got a characteristic Alden White didn't have: Jim's a busybody. As for Frank Bellingham, he's old an' sick, and when I'm that way I'd like to think someone will help me a little. Maybe McGregor's right, it's not part of the constable's job—but whose responsibility is it? No one else seems to give a damn, except for Fred."

She said, "And me—and Bertha."

He looked a little startled. "Bertha?"

"Walt, I told you it is known around town that you have Mr. Bellingham in a cell and he hasn't broken any laws. Bertha told me she knew from the first time she set eyes on you that you were a decent man. . . . Where are we going?"

"Up ahead another mile or so. There's a real pretty place with a spring in the center of it and old trees."

She straightened around to watch the big mare's heavy hips rise and fall in alternating sequence. It was a beautiful night. Out of the clear blue she said, "Do you know Mr. Warren?"

"Yes—well—can't exactly say I know him but I've talked to him a couple of times."

"He asked me to go buggy-riding with him night before last."

Walt's hands tightened slightly on the slack lines. "What did you tell him?"

She laughed. "That I didn't go buggy-riding at night." At the look he gave her she laughed again. "Well, up until tonight it was the truth."

The big mare did indeed know her destination, and when she reached it she cocked her ears back and slackened her gait, waiting for the eased-back lines which would tell her to stop.

Walt removed her bridle so she could pick, hobbled her, and went over where Elizabeth was spreading a red-checkered tablecloth on the grass.

Some astonished frogs that lived at the spring squawked and plopped into the water. A small owl roosting overhead in a cottonwood tree stood it as long as he could; then, as his courage drained, he went flapping wildly away. It was about time for him to start his nightly rodent hunt anyway.

CHAPTER 7
By Moonlight

HE had not anticipated the subject arising, although perhaps he should have. If he'd had any idea it was going to come up he would have been on guard to head it off.

They had eaten and were slouching in weak starshine listening to frogs and crickets when she said, "I didn't think I'd ever do this again; go on a picnic with a man." Her face was gently composed in the soft light. She was looking slightly away from him. "I never thanked you, did I? I've thanked Bertha a dozen times." Her eyes came up to his face. "You were—wonderful, Walt. Everyone was, including Mr. Tower and Mr. O'Bryon. But mostly you and Bertha."

He suspected there were tears close to the surface, so he straightened up a little before speaking. "You're talkin' to an expert about picking up the pieces. Before I came to Peralta it seems that was about all I ever did."

Her interest quickened. "You? The solid rock of granite in the Peralta country?"

He smiled slightly. "I was going to get married." When he added nothing more her interest heightened considerably. "What happened—she died like my husband did?"

"No. I darned near did, of a broken heart. No. She went off with a traveling man out of Kansas City. He peddled bolt goods and corsets and such things. Wore pearl-gray spats and a little curly-brim derby hat to match."

Elizabeth held her hands in her lap like small birds. "I'm sorry, Walt."

He nodded slightly. "Yeah. I was too for a few years. So I drifted. Well, I learned something. If a man goes around feeling like everything has fallen apart, just about everything that can fall apart when he's working will fall apart. I had a horse fall and bust my leg. I caught pneumonia in mid-summer. One blessed thing after another right up until I took the job as constable here in Peralta."

"Things have been better for you?"

"Yes. But I still believe a man with the miseries attracts miseries." He paused, watching her, then added a little more. "This here is the first picnic I been on since before she ran off with that traveling man."

He stood up and held his hands out to her. As she came up beside him he led her to the little spring, and once again a series of splashes signified that the frogs had jumped in. She did not respond to his light grip on her fingers but neither did she withdraw her hand. "I had no idea there would be a spring out here, but then I've never been east of town before."

He smiled. "I'd like to show you the countryside. South of here there is a lot of desert. But northern New Mexico is more like southern Colorado." His smile lingered, but faintly. "I like it here."

She watched frog heads appear on the surface of the small pool, little more than bulging eyes showing. "Bertha loves this country. Do you remember last summer she thought she would go back on a visit to Missouri? She changed her mind. She told me she'd been away so long it wouldn't be the same, and besides that, she has her roots in the Peralta country now." For a moment he thought there was a faint response to his hand before she said, "I understand that. I have nothing to go back to either—and it is a good country with good people in it." This time the squeeze on his hand was defi-nitely noticeable just before she disengaged her fingers from his and turned to look elsewhere.

"The cafe is doing well, Walt. I've just about repaid Bertha for the loan . . . I'll stay."

He led the way over nearer the rig, where the Morgan mare was cropping grass-heads. The moon arrived, lopsided and faintly rusty. Its light increased visibility somewhat; they could see what appeared to be ghostly shadows in the distance, up where foothills and mountains blended. She asked if he'd ever been in the mountains above the Heinz place. He had; he'd hunted up through there each autumn for several years. He told her of ancient stone rings where Indians had made meat for winter.

"Where they had tipis the ground is a little lower than the surrounding ground. There used to be burial scaffolds up there too, but they've fallen down by now."

She was interested. "What happened to them?"

"The Indians? They're gone, that's about all I can tell you. The ones the army didn't corral an' ship to a reservation just sort of faded away up through the mountains. I've heard that some got to Canada, and some still live as hideouts, but so far back in the mountains no one ever sees them. Now and then someone coming down to the Peralta country from the big valleys across the mountains tells about seeing campfire smoke."

She went to stand beside a raffish old cottonwood tree. He thought that by daylight or moonlight she was a beautiful woman. He also thought that perhaps Bertha had been right the first time when she had cautioned him against too much hope, because Elizabeth still remembered things.

He leaned on the big, old mare, who accepted this without bothering to lift her head from the grass. He felt awkward. He also felt slightly cut off from Elizabeth. She left him with a sensation of being not quite part of her existence. He said, "Want to go back now?" and she surprised him. "No, not quite yet. It's so peaceful and quiet out here. Are you in a hurry?"

He almost laughed. "No. I just thought maybe you'd seen enough."

She looked directly at him with a lucid expression. She seemed to understand what was bothering him. She walked over, took his hand in silence, and pulled him with her. They walked slowly, hand in hand, until a ground owl exploded underfoot, leaving its burrow with a mighty leap into the air. She gasped and hurled herself into Walt's arms.

He felt her tremble, but when she looked up she was smiling at him. "Frightened me. What was it?"

"Ground owl," he replied. "They move into abandoned prairie dog holes. He gave me a start too. . . . Did you ever go pheasant hunting, Elizabeth?"

"No."

"Pheasants do that; wait until you're almost atop them, then explode and go flapping away. If you're not used to it they'll get you so rattled you'll miss when you shoot."

He would have continued to hold her, but with both hands against his chest she gently pushed clear.

As they resumed their stroll she said, "That man who asked me to go buggy-riding with him—Mr. Warren . . ."

"What about him?"

"I don't exactly know, Walt. I can't quite define it." She threw him a sidelong, almost apologetic, look. "Female intuition, I suppose."

"You don't like him?"

". . . No. But I can't say why I don't."

He felt for her fingers and held them again as they strolled. "What have you heard about him, Elizabeth?"

Something in his tone made her stop and turn. "Nothing; just that he is going to start up a stage company in town . . . Walt?"

He avoided her gaze. She evidently had not heard about the incident in the livery barn harness-room with the puppy. "Well," he replied lamely, "It looks to me like he travels in pretty rough company. Those two friends of his don't strike me as being church-goin' fellers."

He tugged her, and a short distance farther along they turned back. The big Morgan mare was full of grass-heads and was patiently dozing, standing hipshot in the moonlight. As they came closer she opened one eye, then closed it.

Elizabeth broke the silence with a question. "Do you like the idea of a new stage company in Peralta?"

He had not thought much about it one way or the other. All he knew was that if Fred Tower held out and refused to sell the land Ralph Warren wanted, there might not be a new stage outfit. "We already have one, Elizabeth. It's not much more'n a way station, but so far it seems to get the job done." He remembered Jim McGregor's impassioned conversation out front of her cafe. "I have a feelin' Mr. Warren'll liven things up, make folks take notice of his company. Maybe he'll bring more trade to town."

"Do you favor that?" she asked.

He turned to smile at her. "McGregor sure does. That's what we were talkin' about out front when you came to the door. He's got a real big bee in his bonnet about Warren's new stage company."

"I know. But how do you feel about it? Mr. McGregor told me it will mean progress for Peralta."

His smile lingered. "Something I know for a fact from seeing it happen in other cow-towns, Elizabeth, is that a lot of folks don't know the difference between growth and progress. Progress is fine. Growth for the sake of gettin' bigger usually isn't. Anyway, he wants that piece of ground where Fred Tower had his tannery, and Fred won't sell it to him, so maybe we won't have to worry; maybe Mr. Warren'll go hunt a town that'll do more for him."

She shook her head. "He is going to stay no matter what. He likes Peralta. . . . I wish I understood my feelings about him better."

They went over to the picnic area, cleaned up, took the wicker hamper back with them to the rig, and as Walt was kneeling to remove the hobbles, Elizabeth placed the hamper under the seat and waited. He handed her up, smiled at her, went around to climb in beside her, and talk up the Morgan mare.

The drive back was more leisurely than the drive out had

been. There was a robe in the buggy which he offered her, but she declined. It was not chilly enough yet for a lap robe. He looked at her from the corner of his eye. She was relaxed, head back, her expression peaceful. He said, "Tomorrow night we could maybe get an earlier start and drive up to the foothills over east in the direction of Heinz's range."

She laughed. "Tomorrow night after I close up I have to drain corned beef I've had in a crockery jug for three days, resalt it, and put it to soak again. And after that I have to sew." She watched his profile. "But night after tomorrow night—if you're not too busy—we could go for another drive."

His expression brightened. "A little earlier?"

"Walt, I can't close the cafe before six."

He accepted that. "All right. I'll be along with a rig at ten after six. Maybe this time I can fetch the picnic."

She stared. "You?"

"Well, not me exactly. I'll get Bertha to make something up for us."

She seemed to accept that suggestion. After a while, when they had moonlighted rooftops in sight, she brought up something different. "Would you do me a favor, Walt?"

"You just name it."

". . . Next Sunday when the cafe is closed—would you let me bring the picnic?"

He looked around quickly. Maybe he had been wrong back there at the spring. Maybe Bertha had been right about Elizabeth being ready to pick her life up again. This time she had mentioned buggy-riding, he hadn't. "I'd like that very much," he told her. "Next Sunday . . . Elizabeth, we could get an early start, say maybe about nine or ten o'clock in the mornin', and make a day of it."

She nodded. "Between nine and ten in the morning . . . Now, about that favor."

"I thought goin' buggy-riding next Sunday might be the favor."

"No," she said, quietly, looking steadily at him. "I should have asked you right off. Now I feel a little uncomfortable."

He eyed her warmly. "Just go right ahead and ask it. Elizabeth, as long as we live if you want somethin' and I can possibly get it, all you got to do is—"

"Will you bring old Bellingham along with you when you come after me in the buggy, Walt?"

He was so completely unprepared for this he almost hauled back on the lines. The Morgan mare, with years of experience at guessing moods in two-legged creatures, slackened her gait. When there was no tug, she picked it up again. This close to home and her corral with a bait of feed awaiting her in it, she widened her stride a little.

At the look on Walt's face the handsome woman got a little flustered. "No," she said quickly. "It was just an idea. You don't have to do it . . . I just thought it might be good for him. He doesn't have anyone. I've seen how people treat him . . . It just seemed to me it might help. He's probably having a very hard time of it right now. . . ."

Walt let go a silent, long sigh and nodded. "I'll bring him. We'll need a bigger rig."

"It will put you to more trouble, won't it?"

His recovery was complete by this time. "No. You're right. It should do him a world of good."

They said no more until he turned in out front of the cafe and went around to hand her down. As they walked around in front of the big mare and stepped up onto the plankwalk, she stopped and looked searchingly at him. "I wish I hadn't brought it up, Walt."

He took her hand and murmured something that was not quite true. "I'm glad you did, Elizabeth."

She hesitated at the front door, then abruptly stood up on her tiptoes and kissed him squarely on the lips, turned and disappeared inside the darkened cafe.

He did not bother climbing into the buggy. He led the Morgan mare down the empty roadway to O'Bryon's barn, turned in, and with the wet rumble of snoring coming from the harness-room, took the mare from between the shafts, peeled off her harness, dumped it in the rig, and took the mare out back to her corral. He did not awaken O'Bryon.

There were very few lighted windows in Peralta, none the full length of Main Street as he walked up to the jailhouse to look in on Bellingham, and afterwards to lock up for the night before heading for his quarters at Bertha's place.

Bellingham was wide awake when Walt took a lantern down into the cell-room. The old man raised up on his bunk, wrinkled his eyes against lampglow, and said, "I thought you'd gone home."

Walt hooked the lantern by its bail to a nail in the ceiling and looked solemnly in at the old man. "No. I went buggy-riding. Frank, when was the last time you went on a Sunday picnic?"

Bellingham raised a soiled cuff to his watering eyes before answering. "What time is it?" he asked.

"I got no idea. Maybe nine. What's that got to do with a picnic?"

"Have you been all this time up at the Horseshoe?"

"Frank, I just told you, I've been buggy-riding. You think I'm drunk?"

Bellingham stopped drying his eyes and started scratching his head. "Picnic? What picnic? It's not the Fourth of July already, is it?"

Cutler took a steel bar in each hand and looked irritably in. "I asked you a simple damned question. In return I'm getting a confounded argument."

Bellingham stopped scratching. "The last time I was on a picnic, Mr. Cutler, was a year before the war. My wife an' I went up along a creek near where we lived. That was a long time ago. A hundred years ago, Mr. Cutler."

"Your wife; I never heard you'd been—"

"No reason why you should have heard that I'd been married. I never told anyone I was. She died in the third year of the war when I was somewhere down around Atlanta with Yankees comin' at us from every direction, and I don't want to talk about this."

Walt leaned on the front of Bellingham's cell. "Frank, you're going on a picnic next Sunday. An all-day ride up into the foothills and—"

Bellingham was mopping his eyes again when he interrupted in a thin, harsh voice. "No, I'm not going to do any such a damned thing. I'm not going on a picnic and stir up a lot of memories. No more picnics as long as I live!"

Walt caught his breath. How in the hell had all this happened? All he had intended to do when he had paused to look in on Bellingham was give him something to look forward to. Now what was he going to tell Elizabeth? She wanted this picnic very much. She wanted to . . .

"Constable, go home," the old man said. "Get away from here and leave me alone. You come busting in here in the middle of the night . . . One thing you can do before you go. Fetch the bottle down here. That's the least you can do after what you just done."

Walt eyed the old man for a long moment, then turned on his heel. He did not go near the lower desk drawer. He locked up from outside and went up to his bed at the rooming house.

CHAPTER 8
One Damned Thing After Another!

KELLY O'BRYON hired a new dayman. When he gave Constable Cutler this bit of information over breakfast at the cafe counter, he actually beamed. Walt paid him for the use of the rig the previous night and ignored O'Bryon's news by asking to use the buggy again tomorrow night, and telling him that next Sunday he'd need a spring wagon or something large enough to carry three people and a picnic hamper.

O'Bryon's delight at hiring a replacement for old Bellingham was not to be dampened, not even by talk of business. He said, "All right, you can have the new rig tomorrow night, and on Sunday you can take that light surrey, the one Fred put a new dashboard on. . . . This new man—believe this or not, Walt, he don't drink. An' he's a lot younger than old Bellingham."

"You'll most likely have to pay him in cash money," Walt said with unnecessary sarcasm.

"This feller's new in town. That big feller with the button on the front of his hat—Mr. Warren—he sent this feller down to me accompanied by one of those gunguards who work for Warren. His name is Jack Pinter. He's darn near as big as you are, Walt; strong as an ox. So far he is workin' out fine."

Walt finished his breakfast, paid up, and took two pails of food and coffee across the road to the jail. He did not mention to Bellingham that Kelly had replaced him. In fact, he said very little to the older man, but this time when Bellingham mumbled about the bottle Walt went after it. There was just enough left at the bottom of the bottle for two swallows. Frank downed them in one big swallow, held out the bottle, and said, "You have some more, Constable?"

Walt didn't have. "No. How did you like those eggs with the toast busted up in them?"

Bellingham looked blankly at the empty pail. "Is that what that was?"

Walt swore. "Damned if you make sense to me sometimes, Frank. Those were good eggs. That's what I just had for breakfast at the cafe."

Bellingham went after the pail of black coffee, drained it, and pushed both pails beneath his cell door with one broken old boot. "Constable," he said in a subdued voice. "Mostly, I don't taste food any more. I got some coins; you could get one of those bottles of dregs from Flannery."

"Do you know what's in those bottles Pat Flannery sells you, Frank? Barmen empty whatever is in the bottom of whiskey glasses into a special bottle. Sometimes it's Scotch, sometimes it's malt or rye whiskey, sometimes it 90-proof tequila. You could strip varnish off a table with dregs. It's poison, Frank."

Bellingham's reply came in a fierce thin blur of words running together as he glared at Walt. "You ever had the cold sweats and the shakes, an' a headache like a moose is having a baby inside your head—and maybe fifteen cents to your name. Mr. Cutler, I hate preachers. I got twenty cents in my pocket. I got to have something to drink. *I got to!*"

Bellingham rummaged in his filthy old trousers for the two silver coins as Walt Cutler spoke to him. "I'll make you a trade. I'll get you some whiskey, and you can have two swallows like I've been giving you—and you go on that picnic with Elizabeth Bartlett and me next Sunday."

Bellingham pushed his unsteady fist through the steel bars. "Here. Take the money but for Gawd's sake get me something to drink."

"Did you hear me, Frank?"

"Yes, I heard you. Take the money, Mr. Cutler!"

Walt made no move to take it. "Do we have a trade—you'll go with us next Sunday?"

"Yes. Yes, for crissake. Now take the damned money!"

Walt took it. He also picked up the little pails, returned to the office, and tossed the coins on the desk. Then he went over to the cafe, put the empty pails on the counter and smiled at Elizabeth almost grimly before leaving the cafe on his way up to the saloon.

Pat Flannery was washing glasses in a zinc tub half-full of greasy water. There was not a customer in the place. He looked surprised. "It's kind of early in the morning, isn't it?" he asked.

Walt ignored the question. "Give me a quart of good whiskey, Pat."

Flannery set up the bottle, watched Cutler count out payment for it, then asked another question. "Walt, is this for old Bellingham, because if it is I can tell you that you're wastin' good money. He drinks dregs an' I got three bottles.

Constable Cutler grasped the bottle by the neck. "Pat, if you got a conscience I don't see how you can sell that stuff for people to drink. It's the worst kind of rotgut an' you know it."

Flannery was surprised at the heat of Cutler's statement, but he did not yield an inch. "This here is a saloon, Constable. Folks who buy dregs know as well as you do that it's rotgut. But they want it and pay me for it. I'm not a priest and neither are you."

Walt walked out of the saloon with Pat Flannery's gaze on his back. Pat wagged his head. If people wanted to burn their insides out with rotgut, that was their business, and as far as old Bellingham was concerned, he was too far gone for it to make any difference.

Irritated, Pat went back to the tub full of greasy water and the glasses floating in it. Out front Constable Cutler almost collided with Jim McGregor, his gold watch chain shiny in morning sunlight, his pale, shrewd eyes widening at the sight of Constable Cutler gripping a quart of whiskey in his hand so soon after breakfast. McGregor cleared his throat. "Did you talk to Fred?" he asked, very pointedly ignoring the bottle. "What did he say?"

Walt was still upset. "He said no, he won't sell his land to Warren."

McGregor glanced in the direction of the bank. His clerk was opening up. He brought his gaze back to the constable. "That's real bad," he exclaimed. "Mr. Warren went down to Gloria on the evening stage last night to clinch that arrangement with the mining people. He's been busier'n a cat in a box of shavings getting everything lined up. They're figurin' on moving the first load of bullion in the next few days."

Walt's brows dropped a notch. "Before he's even got a way station up here?"

"Them mining men got a schedule they been stickin' to for several years. Mr. Warren told me yesterday he can't even hope to get that contract from them unless he can slide in right now and commence transporting their bullion. Walt, on something like this a man can't let someone like Fred Tower keep him waiting."

"What about the war wagons, Jim?"

"He's got 'em. Some of his men brought them up as far as Gloria last week. Everything is ready to start." McGregor glanced in the direction of the harnessworks on the opposite side of the road and rested a hand lightly on Cutler's shoulder. "You got to make Fred come to his senses. For the sake of the town and all of us who live in it. You got to." McGregor's eyes dropped to the bottle Cutler was holding. "Take that over there with you." The pale eyes returned to Cutler's face. "An' let me know how you come out. I'll be at the bank." McGregor gave Walt's shoulder a slight squeeze, then he struck out for the bank.

Walt did not cross to the harnessworks; he went down to

the jailhouse and this time he did not take the bottle into the cell-room with him. He measured out two jolts into a tin cup and took that down there.

Bellingham clutched at the cup through the bars, nearly spilled its contents, and threw his head back. He did not swallow twice, he swallowed once. He had perfected a technique of filling his throat and mouth, both, before swallowing. That way he got twice as much whiskey down in one swallow. Walt had never noticed a drinker doing that before, but he had never made a study of drinkers. All his job required of him was that when people got a load on and became troublesome, he was to collar them, lock them up until they were sober, then turn them out.

Bellingham's mouth was open so that he could gulp air.

Walt took the tin cup back and pointed with it. "Go set on the bunk, Frank. Get some sleep if you can. I'll be back directly."

Bellingham turned to obey as he said, "What kind of whiskey was that? It didn't make me feel like heaving."

Walt did not answer. "Lie down. I'll be back at supper time." He returned to the office, tossed the tin cup into a bucket of water behind the stove, stowed the bottle in the same lower desk drawer where he had kept the other one, then walked up to the harness shop.

Kelly O'Bryon was up there to pick up some leather halters Fred had repaired. They were both leaning on the counter as Walt entered. O'Bryon nodded, and Fred did too, but Fred's expression was more speculative than amiable and he said, "I saw you over in front of Pat's place talkin' with McGregor. Did he put you up to talkin' to me?"

Walt sighed, leaned on the counter, and gazed at a saddle clinched onto a stand until the new skirts and jockeys dried into the proper shape. It was the same saddle Gus Heinz had been riding into town for as long as Walt could remember. Walt's delayed reply to Fred's question gave Kelly an opportunity to speak.

"I was just tellin' Fred about my new dayman—Jack Pinter."

Walt nodded indifferently.

"Strange thing happened at the barn a while back," Kelly continued. "Jack dumped his warbag and bedroll in the harness-room an' went out back to pull the wheels off'n that new buggy and slather grease on the axles, an' I kicked his warbag aside so's I'd have room to set at my table to do some bookwork, and a six-gun slid out on the floor. It's got ivory grips an' down the back-strap is six little crosses, inlaid in silver."

Walt turned to slowly regard the liveryman. "What did you do with it?"

"Poked it back into the warbag, cinched up the pucker-string so's it wouldn't slide out again, and come up here to get these halters." As Kelly finished speaking, his eyes remained fixed on Constable Cutler.

Fred Tower broke the short silence, speaking in a dry voice. "We been pondering on things, Walt. You know as well as we do that there aren't no saddlebums willing to dung out livery barns who own guns like that."

Walt, who had forgotten about McGregor, said, "Go on."

"Well, what would you say if you knew a man who packed a gun like that? You'd say he was more than likely a gunfighter. Now then, why would you say he'd be willin' to go to work dunging out someone's barn for nine dollars a month?"

Walt shrugged. His two old friends had obviously been deep in a process of conjecture before Walt had walked in. Not until Fred spoke again did Walt begin to share their suspicions.

"The gent who brought this Pinter-feller down to get hired on to replace old Bellingham. . . . He knew Pinter. They was friends. The feller who brought him down had a knife-scar down the left side of his face."

Walt straightened up. "Jensen?"

Kelly answered. "Yeah. Said his name was Buck Jensen. I

know him and Mr. Warren are friends. I've seen them—and another stranger—around town together. All three of them left town last night on the southbound stage for Gloria. What Fred and I been pondering is—maybe there's somethin' goin' on. Walt, maybe if you talked to this Jack Pinter. . . ."

Constable Cutler gazed thoughtfully at his friends through a long moment of silence. O'Bryon spoke again. "They hired horses off me and spent all day yestiddy riding around the country. I know that because when they brought the horses back they'd been rode, an' not just as far as some shade trees either."

Walt knew what those men had been doing. At least he knew what the banker had told him they had been doing, familiarizing themselves with the countryside and roadways. He fixed Fred with a steady gaze. "The man with the scar, wasn't he in here yesterday when you and the other one got into an argument?"

"Yes. He just stood aside lookin' like he was enjoying things, with a sort of smirkin' smile on his face. He was younger'n Warren and the feller with the weasel eyes. . . . Jensen. Do you know the name of the other one, Walt?"

"Yeah. Herman Smith. He's the one that you got mad at."

Fred lowered his head and looked at the scarred old countertop in what seemed to be concentration. Before he could say anything, Walt asked Kelly if Jack Pinter wore a gun. Kelly had not seen a gun, but he also said that with a gunman, if that was what Jack Pinter was, there was always a possibility that he carried a hideout weapon.

Walt knew that. "Take your halters back down to the barn, Kelly, and find somethin' for that feller to do over across the alley in the wagon shed. Go over there with him, grease axles, put in some new leathers, splice harness—keep him over there and away from the harness-room."

"You goin' to look at that gun?"

"No, not the gun. I want to see what else he's got in his warbag. Keep him out of the barn as long as you can."

Kelly nodded understanding and agreement, took his halters, and left the harnessworks. When Walt also turned to leave, Fred spoke quietly from behind his counter. "Wait. I'll get my ten-gauge and go down there with you."

Walt scowled. "No thanks. You got plenty of work to do."

"Well, I could just sort of step into a stall with my shotgun. He'd never see me."

"Maybe he wouldn't, but you'd have to come out of the stall sometime, Fred; people carryin' shotguns in town start talk. If I need you, I'll send for you. Thanks for the offer anyway."

Fred continued to lean on his counter long after Constable Cutler had departed. He was bothered by his last involvement in one of Constable Cutler's difficulties. That time he had come out of it with a knee the size of a ham, and he had said several times since that the only favor Walt Cutler could ever do him was never again to dragoon him into helping the law.

But still and all, a man had an obligation to help in the maintenance of law and order.

Suddenly, a short, stocky figure filled his doorway. Fred straightened up in surprise to see Bertha Maloney from the rooming house. He was completely baffled by her visit. Bertha did not own a horse, a buggy, or even as far as Fred knew, any riding or driving harness.

CHAPTER 9
An Interesting Day

BERTHA had cinched up her dress in the middle, which made Fred think of squeezing a tomato—the middle shrank and the upper and lower parts pooched out. She smiled as she approached the counter. Fred returned the smile; they had been friends a long time but she never visited the harness shop. Because Bertha Maloney was a direct person she startled Fred when she said, "I heard what you'n the constable are trying to do with old Bellingham and I want to help."

Fred's eyes wandered while he groped for words. Bertha did not give him the chance to find any. She put some old greenbacks on the counter. They looked as though they had been under a brick for a long time; they were pressed flat. "Get him some new britches and a decent shirt, maybe a pair of boots and—because I was married a long time an' know men—get him some new underwear." She paused, watching Fred's face. It was pink under its lifelong tan. "If there's anything left, a haircut and a shave too. Make him take an all-over bath before he puts on new clothes."

Fred eyed the pressed-flat money. "Bertha . . . that'll be from your savings."

"What of it? Money that's been in a dark place under a flat-iron is about as useless as bosoms on a man."

Fred's pink blossomed into bright red, and he did not take his eyes off the money. He cleared his throat. "I don't know, Bertha. I'd have to talk to Walt first."

"Yes. Will you do it?"

He nodded. "Yes'm."

Her dead-level, no-nonsense eyes softened and she smiled. "There is something that I never could fathom about you, Fred. You've never been married?"

"No, ma'am."

"Well—tell me why for heaven's sake. You're a good-lookin' man with an eye to business. As far as I know, you aren't a drinker. I know you chew tobacco, which is a filthy habit, but then I guess someone's got to do it."

She marched out the same way she had come in, erect and deliberate. Fred waited until she was out of sight, then counted the money. There was enough for everything she wanted done. He put the money in a locked drawer and went back to the saddle-rack to see if Heinz's saddle was ready to be finished. It was, so he went to work with neat's-foot oil—from the underside of the leather; never on top of it—and thought about Bertha Maloney. He knew she never minced words. He knew she was a widow. He knew she made money, and now he knew she saved it as well. But what the hell did any of that have to do with her wanting to know why he had never been married?

Outside in the roadway the morning freshness was yielding to heat. By afternoon it was going to be hot. Some boys with piping voices went southward followed by two mongrel dogs with bony tails and panting grins. There was a heat-haze in the distance. It made the mountains appear as apparitions; something that shifted and grew alternately pale and smoky. Autumn could be hot too.

By the time winter arrived, folks would wish they had some of the hot weather back. Jim McGregor shed his coat, draped it over the back of his desk chair, and hauled out his big gold watch, flipped the case open, and studied the delicate black hands shaped as arrows. He closed the watch, lit a cigar, and leaned back as his clerk came up with some ledger sheets. Jim glanced at them and ignored the cough of his clerk, who did not smoke, and reached for a pen to initial each sheet before handing them back as he said, "Fred Tower is giving me indigestion."

The clerk, a wizened, frail man with a chin that receded into his neck, nodded without any expression. He was accustomed to the larger man's candid exclamations.

"He is going to cost Peralta its first decent chance for a new business enterprise worth a damn in fifteen years. Did you know that, Clinton?"

"Well, yes sir, if you say so . . . I was returning from the outhouse across the alley a few minutes ago an' saw somethin' unusual: Constable Cutler hiking up from the lower end of town like he was up to something."

McGregor scowled. "Up to something?"

"He was walkin' so fast he was near to trotting."

McGregor removed the cigar. "A man walkin' fast don't have to be up to something, Clinton. . . . There's somebody at your wicket."

The clerk murmured, "Yes sir," and turned away.

McGregor plugged the stogie back between his teeth, puffed up a big head of smoke, watched his clerk briefly, then scowled at some papers on the desk and went to work.

Several horsemen entered Peralta from the north road riding in a group. McGregor looked up in time to see them pass the bank. A number of other townspeople did the same, and while it was not unusual for rangemen to appear in town in a group like that, it ordinarily only occurred on Saturdays. Still, with rangemen a person could never be very sure of anything. They were like autumn leaves, they came and went, blown along by personal and vocational destinies no one but other stockmen understood, or, for that matter, cared much about.

Walt Cutler missed seeing the riders because he was entering the jailhouse from the back alley when they rode southward. He might not even have paid any attention to them anyway. He had rummaged through Jack Pinter's war bag down at O'Bryon's place and come up with something startling. He sat at his desk and carefully spread the paper in front of him to reread it. Across the top of the paper in large black letters it said WANTED. Below that there appeared what seemed to be an artist's sketch of a man derived from general descriptions. Below this likeness were the words "Five Hundred Dollars Reward Dead or Alive—John Alpen." The crimes supposedly committed by this John Alpen included murder, stage and bank robbery, horse theft, and train robbery.

No particulars were given. Further information, said the wanted poster, would be supplied upon request by the office of the U.S. marshal in Denver, Colorado.

There was no date on the dodger. From its condition Cutler thought it had probably been kept folded in Pinter's war bag for a year or two.

He leaned back, considered the far wall, and decided that although that sketch of John Alpen could have suited a lot of men, it didn't seem entirely reasonable that a man would be hauling his own dodger around for a year or two. In fact, John Alpen would be a fool to haul it around, if indeed Jack Pinter was John Alpen.

The gunfighter's customized handgun was a beautiful weapon, perfectly balanced, with a trigger-pull engineered by a talented gunsmith to give the gun's user a split-second edge. The weapon had cost a small fortune. As for the little sterling silver inlaid crosses down the backstrap and some other inlaid and engraved silverwork—most gunmen avoided anything that ostentatious, but not all of them did. That gun was someone's cherished tool of the trade, and excluding the elegance of the thing, it was understandable that a man who staked his life on his handgun would spare no expense to provide himself with every possible guarantee of survival.

Walt had left the gun in the bag along with the personal effects of the bag's owner. He had considered leaving the dodger too, but in the end appropriated it. There was a possibility that Pinter-Alpen, or whoever he was, might not miss it, or if he did, might not be worried very much over the loss, since such things had a way of falling out during rummagings at camp or in bunkhouses.

He got some coffee from the stove, returned to the desk, and composed a letter of inquiry to the U.S. marshal's office up in Denver, posted it over at the slot in the front wall of the general store, and returned to his office to finish the coffee. Even a prompt reply would not arrive at Peralta before about ten days. Meanwhile, Walt's interest in Kelly's new dayman would continue.

Something was pecking at the back of his mind as he sat at the desk. He was trying hard to pin it down when Elizabeth walked in carrying two grub pails for old Bellingham. She looked a little quizzically at him. "I thought you might have forgotten," she said, placed the pails on his desk, and went back to the doorway. "Six o'clock," she said, and hastened back across to the cafe where mid-day diners were beginning to converge.

Walt eyed the pails. Where in hell had the morning gone? He took the pails down to Frank, and although the older man was actually beginning to have color in his face, he was still irritable. Maybe more so than before.

Walt weathered this and returned to the office for the tin cup of whiskey, but he did not take it down there until he was sure Bellingham had eaten. Even then he did so with reluctance. It was his intention to cut him back to one jolt. Not today, but soon, and that was certainly going to make Bellingham even more disagreeable. He thought of Sunday: how was Frank going to act? The old man had nerves crawling like worms under his hide, and he had his craving. Maybe it would have been better if Walt had not forced Frank to agree to go on the picnic. Walt did not want to inflict old Frank's irritability on Elizabeth.

He took the cup down, accepted it back when Frank had

emptied it, retrieved the little pails, and without a word returned to the office about the time Fred Tower walked in, still trying to get beeswax off his fingers after having rolled and waved tan flax thread.

Fred cocked an inquiring glance, and Walt pointed to the dodger. Fred walked over, still pushing a large red bandana over his fingertips, leaned down, and read.

Walt was standing by the front-wall window when the harnessmaker said, "You get that out of his war bag?" Walt nodded without speaking. "Did you get that fancy gun too?"

"No, I left the gun."

Walt went over to his chair at the desk and sat down. Fred took the chair along the front wall, his favorite, and was now down to using the big bandana to coax drying beeswax from beneath his fingernails. "Is Pinter that there Alpen feller?"

Walt shrugged powerful shoulders. "Your guess is as good as mine. That drawing could be any man who hasn't shaved in a week."

Fred examined his handiwork, stuffed the bandana in a pocket where a third of it hung out, and raised his face in the direction of the desk. "You goin' to fetch him in an' lock him up?"

"First I'm goin' to talk to him. Some men get stubborn as billy goats in a cell, others tell everything they know. What I want from this feller, if he is John Alpen, is information. I'm not goin' to lock him up if I think that'll make him pig-headed."

Fred Tower settled back and fixed the constable with a dusty look. "You been readin' books," he said. "In Texas years back the lawmen didn't read books. Mostly, I expect, because they couldn't, but I'll tell you what they did—they taken a man like this gent from the livery barn, an' they put him in a cell with a lawman built about like you're built, and you know what? . . . Sometimes five minutes later, sometimes up to fifteen minutes later, those gents got to talkin' and couldn't hardly be stopped . . . if their mouths wasn't too bad swollen." Fred smiled without an iota of warmth and continued to gaze at his friend. "It works, Walt."

Constable Cutler knew it worked. "I'll try my way first," he said. "If it don't work, then I'll think of something else."

Fred nodded without a whole lot of satisfaction, then changed the subject. "You got any reason to figure that maybe Bertha Maloney's shining up to me?"

Walt blinked. "Bertha? I got no idea."

"Well, a while back she waltzed in and gave me this wad of money—I got it right here in my pocket." He dug for it and leaned to put it atop the desk. "She said to get old Bellingham new pants, underduds, boots, shirt, a bath, shave, and shearing. And she wanted to know why I never got married."

"All in the same breath?"

Fred had to consider that for a moment. "Well, not quite, but pretty close."

"What did you tell her?"

"I said I'd talk to you about Bellingham. I didn't know what to say about the rest of it, an' she didn't give me much of a chance; she went waltzing out of the shop."

Walt kept his eyes on the money, allowed no break in the seriousness of his expression, and did not say a word until he was sure he could do it without laughing. "You know her as well as I do. . . . She's motherly. Look how she took care of Elizabeth last summer after her husband died out there on the homestead. Some women are like that; they got to be mothering things."

Fred arose. "Well for Crissake! Mothering? Me?" He stamped out of the office leaving Constable Cutler looking out into the roadway because Fred had not closed the door after himself.

A little later Walt went over to the emporium to ask the aged clerk with the black sleeve protectors that covered his shirtsleeves from the wrist to the elbow if he knew Frank

Bellingham. The clerk made a little sniffing sound and nodded. "Yes. What about him?"

"Would you know what size britches and shirt and under-duds, socks, and boots he'd wear?"

The clerk fixed Constable Cutler with a doubting expression. "Old Bellingham? Where is he goin' to get the money to pay for them things?"

Walt drew Bertha's greenbacks from a pocket and held them out without saying a word until the clerk's expression changed slightly, then he said, "Can you make a good guess about the sizes?"

The old man could. "Yep. I been doin' that for fifty years." He raised small, shrewd eyes. "Constable, if that's old Bellingham's money—where do you expect he got it? Not from Kelly, for a darned fact, and—"

Walt leaned on the counter looking dispassionately at the clerk. "I didn't know when a body came in here to buy somethin' they had to explain how they got the money to pay with."

The clerk was chastened. He walked briskly from behind the counter, heading for the opposite side of the large, poorly lighted room with its smell of floor oil, cloves, leather, and tobacco smoke. "I got to know the colors and such like, Constable," he said, sounding very professional. "Maybe old Bellingham—"

"His name is Frank. Frank Bellingham."

The clerk turned and eyed Cutler briefly, then shrugged thin shoulders. He had heard, as had just about everyone else, that Constable Cutler was using the jailhouse to dry out old Bellingham, and, as the constable had just implied, it wasn't any of the clerk's damned business.

He cleared his throat and did not use Bellingham's first name; he said, "All right, Constable, *Mister* Bellingham," in a tone of voice that did not conceal the sarcasm. "We got shirts in white, blue, and striped green. We got pants in black, brown, an' buckskin colors."

CHAPTER 10
Toward a Distant Place

FRANK BELLINGHAM was so flabbergasted when Walt told him they were going across the alley to the washhouse so the older man could take an all-over bath he just stared, then he got red. "Since when has a jailhouse occupant got to—"

"Frank, you smell like a billy goat, and I'm not going to argue every time I come down here. Now get your carcass up this corridor." Walt was mindful of the passing of time. He was not going to be late for the buggy-ride with Elizabeth tonight if he had to drag Bellingham over there and personally use the horse-brush on him.

Frank marched up as far as the office and had his back to Walt, staring at the bundles atop the desk until Walt kicked the cell-room door closed and gave Bellingham a rough shove toward the storeroom, beyond which was the alleyway door.

In the washhouse Walt was appalled at the emaciated body, but he said nothing as they hauled water for the tub. It was not warm water. Walt tossed the horse-brush in along with a chunk of brown soap and pointed. "Get in—and scrub!"

Bellingham gasped but got down into the water. He had been thinking fairly clearly this past week; he knew that the expression on the constable's face reflected a no-nonsense approach to this unusual situation. And he scrubbed. He even used the rice-straw brush on his head. When he stood up, Walt tossed him the tattered gray towel and then went to stand in the doorway studying the position of the sun while Frank dried off.

The sun was still high enough; he would not be late.

When Frank was dressed and ready to return to the jailhouse, Walt led the way. In the office, without speaking or scarcely more than looking around, he tossed the new underclothes to Bellingham. Next came the britches, socks, new blue work-shirt, boots, and a new blue bandana handkerchief. Finally, Walt handed him the boots and pointed to a wall bench. Bellingham sat down and took off his old clothes. He put on new socks first, then the boots. He looked up. "Why did you do this?"

Cutler's reply was curt. "I didn't. Someone else did. Now let's go back to the cell—and Frank—no whiskey after supper tonight."

Bellingham did not seem to have heard. He tested the boots before returning to his cell. When the door was locked between them, he looked steadily at Constable Cutler. "I want to pay for these things."

Walt nodded. "Sure you do. I'll be back directly with your supper."

"Constable . . ."

Walt walked up the corridor without answering, closed the door, and crossed over to the cafe for Bellingham's supper.

There were only two diners at the counter because it was too early for the local bachelors to be showing up. Elizabeth handed him the pails with a slight smile and a shy look. He winked and walked back across the road, down into his cell-room, shoved the pails under the door, and looked sternly at Bellingham. "Eat, then sleep."

Frank seemed to want to speak, to perhaps ask questions or show irritability, but Walt walked away before anything could be said between them.

On the way down to the livery barn Walt blew out a big breath. One damned thing after another. If he hadn't had Frank Bellingham in his jailhouse he would have felt better. He had a feeling that Jack Pinter was not going to open up very much, and if he did not—or perhaps even if he did—

Walt might have to put him into one of his cells and he would have preferred having Pinter as his only prisoner.

Kelly was leaving the barn on his way up to the cafe for supper when he and the town constable met in late-day, slanting sunshine. Kelly smiled. "I didn't forget. I got Jack pullin' the rig inside to be hitched up." Kelly looked over his shoulder. The runway was empty. He turned back and dropped his voice to little more than a whisper. "What did you find in his war bag?"

"We can talk about it in the morning," Walt replied and brushed on past. Kelly looked briefly after him, then went hiking on a diagonal course in the direction of the cafe.

Pinter glanced up as Constable Cutler appeared in the rear runway opening. He was pulling the rig. Walt moved in to lend a hand. As he joined the hostler with the rig he said, "How are you and Kelly getting along?"

Jack Pinter, who was a large, powerful-looking man with blue eyes, blond hair, and a set of youngish features, answered casually. "All right. He ain't hard to work for. The pay ain't the best, but then a man can stay inside in the shade if he wants to. Kelly don't seem to mind . . . He said to pull this rig inside and put that big Morgan mare between the shafts. He didn't say who it was for . . . you, Constable?"

"Yes."

Pinter did not speak again until they were inside with Walt holding up the shafts while Pinter backed Big Daisy between them. Then Pinter's grin showed. "This is a pretty fancy rig for a man to use when he's goin' drivin' by himself, ain't it?"

Walt grinned back. "I expect it would be, if a man was going by himself. I'm not."

He helped Pinter harness the big mare. As usual, she was as docile as a lamb. Walt had a question for the hostler. "I haven't seen Mr. Warren or his gunguards around town lately. Did they give up on us here in Peralta?"

Pinter kept his eyes on the leather as he answered. "Naw. Mr. Warren had business down south. Jensen and Smith tagged along."

"They're coming back?"

This time Jack Pinter's reply was slow arriving and sounded guarded. "I think so. They got to if they're goin' to get the new stage company set up." He looked at Walt across the big mare's back. "Mr. Warren's not exactly happy about that feller who owns the harnessworks not sellin' him a piece of land he's got to have."

"Yeah, so I've been told. But I wouldn't worry too much about that. I think Mr. Warren'll get the land in the end. . . . You're a friend of Buck Jensen?"

"Yeah. We rode together years back. Down along the border. Buck's a tophand."

"Were you surprised when you showed up in Peralta and saw him here?"

"Well, not exactly. I heard he was up here." Pinter suddenly walked up to the mare's head to lead her out into the front roadway. Walt's impression was that he did not want to answer any more questions.

Walt trailed the rig. When it stopped in coppery late-day sunshine he went around, accepted the lines, and started to climb up as he said, "Much obliged, Jack."

The big hostler nodded. "Any time, Constable . . . Mind your manners tonight." He laughed and went back down into the barn.

Peralta was preparing itself for the end of this day. Stove smoke was flattening out thinly over town because there was no breeze to carry it away.

The roadway was almost empty; merchants were getting ready to lock up for the night. Northward, showing more pink than tan, dust hung in a long streamer behind the southbound stagecoach coming down toward town.

Elizabeth was not quite ready so Walt had a cup of coffee while he waited. The store clerk walked in despite the cardboard sign on the door that said the cafe was closed for the day. He had a cranky look on his face until he saw Constable Cutler sitting at the counter; then, without a word he reversed himself and went stiffly in the direction of the

Horseshoe, where the purchase of a large glass of beer entitled the drinker to put together a sandwich from among the sausages, thick slices of coarse bread, and other edibles at the far north end of the bar.

When Elizabeth appeared, her face was flushed, her hair had been brushed until it shone, and in Walt's eyes she looked like a schoolgirl. He took the hamper from her and led the way outside. Dusk was on the way but they cleared the upper end of town before it arrived, and this diminishing but still quite adequate visibility permitted a number of people to watch the elegant little rig go past with the constable driving and that widow-woman from the burned-out homestead up in The Neck at his side.

He knew where he was going, which neither Big Daisy nor Elizabeth knew. He did not leave the road, although he yielded the right-of-way to the stagecoach and returned the high wave the driver threw as they passed. There was almost no dust now, because this close to Peralta the whip had his hitch down to a slogging trot.

Elizabeth looked at Walt and said, "How was your day?"

He shrugged. "About like most of 'em."

"Did you give Mr. Bellingham his new clothing?"

He looked at her. "Bertha told you?"

"Yes."

He turned back to watch the big mare. "I gave them to him."

"Did you make him bathe first?"

Walt laughed. "She didn't leave anything out, did she? Yes, I made him take a bath. He was so dumbfounded he didn't even whine about a jolt of whiskey." He paused, then also said, "Elizabeth, maybe it wasn't such a good idea taking him with us Sunday. He's cranky. I don't want anything to spoil our day together."

She reached impulsively and put one hand on his arm. "He won't spoil it." She removed the hand and also gazed up the road. "I think drying out's very hard on him, isn't it?"

"Yeah. But he's beginning to look human again. His

thoughts don't seem to get all scattered when he talks now, and he's eating well." He faced her again, mouth pulled into a wry look. "I'm not sure I ever should have got mixed up in this. There'll be talk around town."

She nodded about that. "There already is. Mostly, the talk I've heard at the cafe is that you're doing a good thing. I had no idea how much feeling there was for someone like Mr. Bellingham among—well—at least the people who eat at the cafe. Jim McGregor seems noncommittal but I know he doesn't approve. That is one man out of about ten or fifteen."

Walt said, "McGregor's a banker. He can't think any other way. If Frank gets lined out, McGregor will tell you he always wanted to help."

They laughed. Walt was nearing the foothills, at least the road became uneven in a tilting way, although there were still level places to be traversed. Elizabeth was looking west, her face set in a composed expression. Walt guessed she was thinking of the homestead, which was roughly due west. He did not interrupt her thoughts but he turned off the road-bed, driving easterly with the faint scent of pine and fir sap in the dusky evening. They were on Gus Heinz's range. There were small bands of cattle and a few horses out a mile or so from the timber. The horses watched them without much interest but as soon as the cattle saw them, they fled, running like scorpions, with tails over their backs. Heinz had worked them through his corrals only a week or ten days earlier. Because of this terrifying experience they would not return to their normal phlegmatic behavior for another two or three weeks.

Walt drove up a broad, flat opening in the trees to a tumbledown log house with a sway-backed horseshed out behind it. When they stopped to alight, a pair of wood rats as large as house cats fled through the doorless front opening. Elizabeth tried not to show her aversion but she was standing so erect that Walt sensed her anxiety.

He took her east of the old log cabin, where honeysuckle

grew with flourishing abandon near a sump-spring. She was surprised to find geraniums growing there until he explained that this was where Gus Heinz and his wife had lived when they had first come into the Peralta country with everything they owned either tied to the tailgate of a wagon, inside it, or out front of it in heavy harness. His wife had cultivated flowers around the sump-spring. What Elizabeth saw was all that remained of her flowers.

"A long time ago," he said, putting the wicker hamper on the grass.

Elizabeth walked over to smell the honeysuckle, though that was not really necessary because in the utter stillness of dusk—without a breath of air stirring—it was possible to detect the fragrance from a considerable distance.

He cared for the Morgan mare, gave her a light pat, and strolled over to Elizabeth. She was standing with both hands clasped in front gazing at something a few yards distant, beyond the soft ground and green grass.

She turned as he approached her. He nodded toward the small wooden headboard set amid mortared rocks and said, "Gus's little daughter. She died when she was a year old. All his children were born in that log house."

Elizabeth turned back toward the small grave. "And his wife, Walt?"

"She died here too, shortly before he and the boys finished the big main house over where the ranch headquarters is."

"It is so sad, Walt."

He agreed. "Yes. You know Gus; he's not a man who talks about personal things. One time he told me his world ended the day his wife died. But ten years after she died he had put together one of the biggest and best cow outfits around. . . . We used to play poker once a week. Gus, Jim McGregor, Fred Tower, Kelly O'Bryon, and I. He and I sat around after the others had left one night and had a few drinks. He told me he's always had trouble learning, but one thing he learned after his wife died was that he couldn't just go on grieving. He had to do something—anything—so he went ahead and made the ranch he and his wife had talked so much about."

"Walter . . . ?"

He turned to her.

"I know what you're doing," she said quietly.

He did not deny it. His face was gentle in the quiet dusk. "I've never been where you and Gus have been. Is he right or isn't he?"

She looked past him toward the buggy and the big, dozing Morgan mare. "He's right."

Walt led her over to the picnic hamper and helped her spread the groundcloth. She looked up once, and he was watching her. She began removing plates and pails from the hamper and did not look at him again until they were eating. This time when their eyes met, he spoke very seriously.

"I want to ask you something, Elizabeth. The trouble is—I got it worked out how to ask it—what I don't have worked out is when."

He probably could not see her expression in the dusk, and even if he had, he might not have understood it. But the way she stopped moving and sat utterly still, gazing directly at him, would have signified volumes to another woman, and perhaps even to a more experienced man.

He was waiting for her to speak.

She was quiet a very long while. Even when she eventually spoke he had to strain to catch the words. "I don't think I know when the right time is either, Walt . . . but . . . ten years would be an awfully long time. Do you want to ask your question tonight?"

"Yes. Elizabeth, I've been in love with you since those bad days right after your husband died . . . I want to ask you if you would marry me?"

The hesitation he expected did not materialize. She answered him moments after he asked the question. "Yes, I'll marry you. You've been a . . . I've been tormented by what

I've felt for you for a long time. It didn't seem proper. In fact I'm sure it wasn't proper."

He arose slowly, holding his hands out to her. As she came up off the ground he said, "It is proper. I think this last year for you equals Gus's ten years."

The big Morgan mare cocked a drowsy eye in their direction, and a slightly fuller moon than the one they had been beneath the last time they had gone buggy-riding appeared from behind a cloud to heighten visibility considerably. Walt held her to him without pressure and without any demands.

CHAPTER 11
A Hard-Handed Meeting

FRANK BELLINGHAM'S irritability rolled off Constable Cutler like water off a duck's back. Walt smiled through the older man's garrulousness and allowed him his one double swallow of whiskey after he had eaten breakfast. Bellingham's complaint was that it was impossible to get the maximum effect from a big jolt of whiskey on top of a full stomach, and Walt agreed with him. That was part of Walt's strategy. He knew almost nothing about drying out drunks, but he knew enough to experiment. He'd had drunks in his cells who had hallucinated after being deprived of whiskey. He had assumed Frank Bellingham might be someone who would also do that. His response had been to follow a course of gradual temperance. Not to deprive Bellingham completely, just to cut his alcohol back and leave the rest of it to the future.

He'd had Bellingham in the jailhouse about a week now, and to someone who had known the old man before that, and over the years, the change in him was not miraculous, but it certainly was noticeable.

When Bellingham looked venomously out through the bars, Walt smiled at him. When he bitterly complained about being held in jail when he had broken no laws, Walt sympathized without offering to free him. And when Bellingham said he would like a haircut, Walt got the town barber—a short, thick man married to a short, thick, swarthy woman—to bring his utensils to the jailhouse.

The barber had a strong European accent. He used scissors with a flourish, and he encouraged conversation on any subject, although politics seemed of most interest to him.

Somehow he got off on the subject of the Civil War, and Walt saw Bellingham straighten on the stool and flatten his wide, lipless mouth.

But the barber, who had immigrated to the country only after that war, came out in favor of the Confederacy. Bellingham loosened up a little. Walt went back up to his office with the sound of their compatible conversation following him.

Walt's intention was to get Jack Pinter to his office, peaceably if possible, violently if he had to. He had become convinced last night at Kelly O'Bryon's barn that Pinter would never volunteer anything about himself, and Walt wanted to learn as much as possible about Ralph Warren and his gunguards while the three of them were not around.

The opportunity arrived unexpectedly when Kelly came rushing in to say Pinter and a freighter who had parked his big wagon in the alley behind the barn were yelling at each other down yonder.

"His wagon is blocking the rear exit of the barn," Kelly stated. "I went out back to ask him to move it so's we could go in and out, and he got mean. Jack took it up when I left. I could hear 'em yellin' back an' forth before I got out front to come up here."

Walt arose from the desk, reaching for his hat as he asked if either of them was armed. Kelly said that Jack wasn't and he had seen no gun on the freighter.

They left the jailhouse and were two-thirds of the way to the barn when they heard the shouting out back. Over at the blacksmith's shop, which was opposite the barn and north a few yards, both the smith and his helper were in their doorway looking and listening. When they saw Kelly and Constable Cutler hurrying along, the smith said something to his helper. They both started across the road as Walt and Kelly entered the runway.

The freighter was a shaggy, graying, heavy-boned man with a mean face. He was standing at the head of his lead horses, red in the face. Pinter was in the runway opening,

fists clenched. As Walt approached, the freighter called
Pinter a fighting name, and the hostler started for him.

Walt yelled at them. He might as well have whispered.
Neither the freighter nor Jack Pinter could see or hear
anything but each other. The freighter stepped away from
his horses and took a wide stance, big arms up and ready.
Pinter did not even slow his advance. Neither man was
making a sound now.

Walt left Kelly standing nearby and strode toward the
middle of the alley. The freighter saw him coming, saw the
badge on his shirt, and ignored both as he allowed Pinter to
approach within ten feet, then hurled himself forward.
Pinter stopped dead in his tracks, fists rising. The freighter
was old, probably more experienced at brawling. He fetched
up short just beyond Pinter's reach and jettisoned a spray of
tobacco juice that struck the hostler's boots. Pinter roared
and lunged ahead. The freighter was waiting. He had done
that deliberately to bring the younger man to him. It worked
very well. As Jack Pinter came in swinging, the freighter
sucked back and shuffled a couple of feet to his right. He
fired a sledgehammer strike, but Pinter leaned far to his
right, and the big fist barely grazed him.

Walt stopped to wait and watch.

The freighter cursed Pinter again and shifted around to
his right again. Pinter had to get untracked to face him, and
that too was part of the older man's strategy. While the
younger man was moving his feet and turning his body, the
freighter came at him. Pinter did not have time to gather
himself. He took the freighter's second strike directly over
the heart. Walt saw Pinter's legs loosen a little, but he had
youth on his side; his recovery was almost instantaneous. He
dropped low, hit the freighter in the soft parts, got back to
avoid another of those sledging strikes, and within moments
had fully recovered from being struck in the chest.

The freighter was circling to the right again. He passed
within ten feet of Walt without even glancing at him. Pinter
was coming in again. The freighter waited until the last

possible moment, then sprang straight at the younger man. Pinter threw his arms up but the freighter hit him in the stomach. The man could hit like a kicking mule, and this time Jack Pinter's legs bent at the knees.

The freighter went after him. Each time one of his blows landed, Pinter wilted a little more. Finally, when the freighter shuffled back and straightened up to measure Pinter for the knock-down, Walt stepped up, knocked the freighter's cocked right arm aside, and spun the man toward him with his other hand. The freighter did not stagger; he moved on the balls of his feet. He lashed out with his left hand. He could hit hard and he was very fast.

Walt pressed the man. They were about the same height. The freighter had perhaps an inch or two advantage in height, but when he hit the constable over the heart as he had done Jack Pinter, Walt did not even slacken his advance, and the freighter then tried his right-sidling maneuver again. Walt had seen him do this, remembered every move the man made, and stepped to his left to block the freighter's movement. He leaned back to feint the freighter, but evidently the freighter had learned about being pulled in; he refused to be feinted.

Walt paused, waited for the other man to move, and when he started to sidle in the opposite direction, to his left, Walt dodged more quickly, blocked him, and hit him alongside the head when they were close enough.

The freighter's eyes snapped open and closed several times. Walt moved directly at the man. This time he struck him twice, once in the middle and again in the shoulder as the freighter was trying to turn away. The second blow punched the freighter off balance, and Walt gave him no chance to recover, then pressed in with his left arm extended to keep his adversary off balance, his right hand cocked high.

The freighter turned to face Cutler head on, which was a mistake. Walt fired his poised right fist, and the freighter collapsed with a squeezed-out explosion of breath.

O'Bryon, the blacksmith, and the blacksmith's helper were like statues in the runway opening. Jack Pinter slid over to the nearest big freighter-wheel and leaned on it. He was gray beneath his sweaty tan.

Walt ignored the face-down freighter and considered Pinter. "Come on up to my office," he said. "You look like you need some fixing up."

Pinter ignored the constable to gaze dispassionately at the unconscious man. "Get some water," he said very quietly. "Kelly—someone—get a bucket of water and bring that son of a bitch around. I'm goin' to kill him."

The bystanders were looking at the constable and did not move. Pinter shoved off the wheel, shouldered past the men in the barn opening, and strode purposefully in the direction of the harness-room. Kelly and Walt exchanged a look. Kelly was alarmed. He knew where his hired man had gone and why he had gone there. So did Walt.

Walt pushed past the men and walked up the runway. At the harness-room door he stopped. Pinter had a shellbelt and holstered Colt in his hand. He ignored Walt to swing the belt around his middle. He was buckling it when Walt walked into the smelly little room and said, "Forget it! No guns!"

Pinter's eyes were fixed in an unalterable expression. He ignored Walt, buckled the belt, and leaned to secure the holster's tie-down to his leg.

Kelly O'Bryon had been a few steps behind Walt and now stood in the doorway without saying anything.

Walt took two forward steps and reached for the ivory-handled, silver-inlaid six-gun. Pinter struck his hand away as he was straightening. He finally spoke to the constable. "Get out of my way. You think I'm goin' to let that mangy son of a bitch get up and walk away from here?"

Walt's answer was short. "Yeah. That's exactly what you're goin' to do. That fight is finished."

Pinter's icy gaze focused on Walt. He stood a long moment staring, then he gently shook his head. "Not on your lousy life," he said softly, never blinking.

Walt leaned with his left hand moving toward the holstered Colt. When Pinter struck savagely at it this time, Walt
came up from belt-buckle high with his right fist. The sound
was of bone against solid bone.

Jack Pinter went down in a heap, and because the tie-down
was not in place, when he struck the floor and rolled, his
elegant six-gun slid from its holster and stopped against the
wall.

Kelly moved to retrieve the gun and gave it to Walt, who
flexed his sore hand. If this kind of thing continued, he
would need to keep his right hand supple, not hampered by
swollen knuckles.

He stooped over and raised up with the younger man
slung over his shoulder. As he left the harness-room he said,
"Kelly, see if you can get some help and bring that freighter
up to the jailhouse."

It was the busy time of morning along both plankwalks
and out in the road. Walt paid no attention to the stares or to
the pedestrians who got quickly out of his way as he walked
up to the jailhouse. He set Pinter on a bench and propped
his upper body against the wall. Then he tossed the silver-
mounted gunfighter's weapon on his desk, and went after a
long drink of water.

By the time the blacksmith, his helper, and Kelly O'Bryon
arrived with the groggy freighter, Walt had soaked both
hands and was standing by his desk. He opened the cell-
room door and had the freighter taken to a cell and locked
in, under the astonished gaze of Frank Bellingham. Then
Walt returned to his office and thanked the men who had
brought the freighter.

After they departed Walt went back to the water-bucket to
soak his hands again. He was still soaking them when Pinter
groaned and flopped against the wall, groping with his
hands along the bench where he was sitting.

Walt dried off, got his whiskey bottle, and helped Pinter
swallow until he coughed, then Walt put the bottle back and
sank down at the desk to wait.

Pinter recovered slowly. When his eyes were finally focusing, he raised a hand to explore his painful jaw. He opened and closed his mouth, moved his lower face from side to side, finally looked over at Constable Cutler and let go an uneven, long breath. "What the hell happened, Constable?"

"I hit you."

Pinter's eyes widened slightly. "*You* hit me? I thought it was that freighter."

"That fight was over. I hit you because you went after your gun to kill the freighter." Walt picked up the weapon and turned it slowly as he examined it. He fixed Jack Pinter with a cold look. "You won this gun in a poker game," he said, not phrasing it as a question.

Pinter was still gingerly feeling his jaw when he answered. "Yeah. In a poker game."

Walt put the gun down and leaned on his desk. "Every two-bit gunfighter I've ever disarmed said that. An awful lot of men must lose an awful lot of guns like this in poker sessions."

Pinter stopped moving his jaw, lowered his hand to his lap, and looked steadily across the room. "I don't give a damn whether you believe me or not, Constable." Pinter leaned to arise, and Walt growled at him.

"Sit right where you are."

Pinter stopped moving. He studied the harsh expression on Walt's face for a moment before speaking again. "I didn't start that fight. He blocked the alley with his wagon and—"

Walt interrupted in a soft tone of voice. "Alpen. Did you ever hear of a man named John Alpen?"

This time Pinter eased back slowly until his back was against the wall again. If he was surprised it did not show, but his gaze at Walt Cutler was very clear and lucid now. He watched the constable take the dodger from a drawer and spread it flat atop the desk.

When Walt looked up, Jack Pinter's bruised, swelling face was expressionless.

CHAPTER 12
Answers

SINCE Pinter could not see the face-up poster in front of Constable Cutler, it might have been instinct that warned him to remain silent. He might even have guessed about the poster.

Walt looked steadily across the room through an interval of bleak silence. He had not known what to expect when he mentioned what he suspected was Pinter's real name, but he had rather thought it might be something other than silence. Walt said, "You've been busy. What sticks in my craw is the robberies—banks and stages. I'd like to hear the details."

Pinter continued to sit staring at Cutler without saying a word. The constable picked up the gun again, balanced it in his hand, and smiled slightly. The weapon had perfect balance. He did not try dry-firing it; that kind of a weapon would have minimal spring-tension. It was purely and simply a killer-gun.

He raised his eyes to meet the gaze of his prisoner, faint smile intact. Without visible effort he turned the gun gently, pointed it directly at the man across the room, and while still wearing that illusive smile, cocked the six-gun and settled a thick finger inside the trigger guard.

Pinter's eyes went lower, to the gun, to the muzzle aimed directly at him from the width of the room, and to the finger curled inside the trigger guard. He swallowed, and one hand felt for the edge of the bench and gripped the wood.

Walt closely watched each change in Jack Pinter. When he thought his prisoner might be considering alternatives to being shot, Walt snugged his finger until it barely touched the trigger.

Pinter said, "Be careful, you damned fool. That thing'll go off."

Walt moved his bent finger a little more, this time a fraction of an inch away from the trigger, but from across the room the finger could have been moving farther back, not forward.

Pinter made an abrupt gesture with his hand. "For Crissake don't put any pressure on that trigger!"

Walt moved his finger again, his smile gone now. He said, "Talk, Alpen."

Pinter swallowed again, harder this time. "Talk about what?"

Walt let a moment pass before replying. "You know what about. An' if you lie, I'll kill you for tryin' to escape. . . . Alpen, I know more about you and your friends than you suspect. Now—five seconds and you'd better be talking by the end of it."

Pinter began to sweat. He stared at the bent finger as though it fascinated him to the exclusion of everything else, and it probably did. It was his weapon; he knew better than anyone how little pressure had to be exerted against that trigger for the gun to fire. He half-whispered something as he forced his gaze up to Constable Cutler's face. "You wouldn't do it," he murmured, and Walt answered in a quiet but convincing tone, "Yes I would. In a damned minute. I've never had a prisoner escape. You won't either. People in this town will believe I shot you for trying to attack me and bust out. Alpen, you only got a second left."

". . . What do you want to know?"

"Let's start with you taking the job with Kelly O'Bryon."

"I needed a job. I was broke when—"

"You are lying, Alpen."

Pinter checked his flow of words, hesitated, then began over. "They'll hunt me down no matter how long it takes."

"Your five seconds is up."

"Wait, dammit! Give me a little time."

"No. You had your time." As he said this, Walt's big shoulders hunched slightly, he shifted the gun barrel an inch until it was centered on the fugitive's chest.

"Hold it," cried John Alpen. "I took the job with O'Bryon so's I'd be in Peralta if anything went wrong down south, an' if it did an' I saw you gettin' up a posse, I'd be in a position to turn every damned livery horse loose and chouse them away from town."

Walt nodded. "Whose idea was that?"

"Paul's. Paul Lightle, the feller you know as Ralph Warren."

"Tell me about him, Alpen."

The large, muscular outlaw with the youthful features and small head finally looked away from the man with the gun, let his eyes wander briefly then return as he began speaking. "Constable, you know what will happen to me if—?"

"I know what will happen to you if you don't keep on talking, John. Tell me about Mr. Warren."

"You ever heard of Paul Lightle, Constable?"

Walt did not think he had. "Maybe. You refresh my memory."

"He's a puke. You know what that is?"

"Yes. Someone from Missouri. Go on."

"I don't know whether it's true or not, but he told us one time in camp that he rode with the Youngers on some bank robberies. . . . I know one thing for a fact: Paul is a clever man. He never led us into no bank an' he never took us alongside a railroad train. He'd buy tickets an' we'd ride like regular passengers until he give a signal, then we'd jerk the emergency cord to stop the train, shoot open the mail-car door, pitch out the money from the safe, and get the hell away."

"In the middle of nowhere?"

"Naw. He'd stop the train where we'd hid our horses. Usually in some timber. We never even got chased very much. Then we'd split up like we done this time, and sort of drift together again like he'd planned for us to. This time in Peralta. Maybe two or three months later."

"How did he rob banks without entering them?"

"We'd wait for the money-coach, waylay it, and take the bank's money. I know what you're goin' to say: how did we know which stage was carryin' back money? Only thing I can tell you about that is one time after we'd stopped a bullion coach, got clean out of the country, an' was loafin' in a mountain-camp, Paul told us that for five hundred dollars he could bribe a bird down out of a tree. I told you, Constable, he'a real savvy individual. I never asked questions. Neither did Buck or Herman. A man'd be a fool to when someone was puttin' money into his pocket with damned little risk."

Walt lowered the gun muzzle so that it was now aimed at Pinter's middle. "Is that their real names? Herman Smith and Buck Jensen?"

Pinter nodded. "Yeah. Me, I got dodgers out. They do too, but back East somewhere. Paul didn't care about them usin' their real names but he'd give me a different name each time we'd go on a raid."

Walt waited until the fugitive had sleeved sweat off his forehead and upper lip before speaking again. "Is it the bank this time—the one here in Peralta?"

Pinter shook his head. "All that about settin' up a stage company here, gettin' the Peralta banker goin' ahead full steam to help Paul start up—I told you, he's a smart man. . . . That was pure bull from start to finish, but Paul's got a way with folks. He's slicker'n a greased pig."

Walt eased the hammer down on the gun, put it down, and arose to go shove kindling into the pot-bellied stove. He did not say a word until he had a little fire going and had placed the speckled-ware coffeepot atop it. Then he returned to the desk, sat down, and leaned both elbows atop the wood, one on each side of Pinter's gun, and stared at the prisoner.

Pinter was still sweating but he seemed less tense than he had been. In fact as he returned Constable Cutler's impassive stare, he smiled. "You never had no idea, did you?" he asked.

Walt ignored the question to phrase one of his own. "What is it this time—bullion shipments from that mine down below Gloria?"

Pinter's reply suggested that he was becoming reconciled to being found out. "Yeah."

"How do they figure to do it?"

Pinter got more comfortable on the bench as he spoke. "This time Paul give it a lot of thought. He had some counterfeit papers made up showin' him to be representing some rich investors back East. One of 'em was the president's brother. He put a lot of money in the bank down at Gloria— then he went down to that mine and got those gents interested because he said he could move their bullion up to Denver cheaper an' faster than they been movin' it . . . Constable, like I said, Paul can talk a bird down out of a tree."

"How did he figure to move it?"

"In two war wagons. We bought them down near Nogales, drove 'em up to Gloria, and—"

"Who drove them to Gloria?"

"Some Mexicans he hired. Then they went back down south. That's why he took Buck an' Herman down there with him day before yesterday. To drive the rigs."

"That's all, just Herman and Buck?"

"Yes. I was to meet them when Paul sent word up here by the northbound morning stagecoach, an' if you hadn't got wind of anythin' by then, I was to ride south and meet 'em somewhere below Gloria on the way to Mexico. Did you ever hear of anything slicker'n that?"

Walt did not say whether he had or not. The coffee was boiling. He drew off two cups, handed one to his prisoner, and returned to the desk with the other one. "Mexico," he murmured, sitting down and leaning forward on the desk. "John, either you're lying or he's not so smart if he figures to go down into Mexico with a couple of wagons loaded with bullion. Mexicans'll kill a man for his horse, for his boots, sometimes just for his hat . . . An' they know what war wagons are used for."

Pinter listened, pinched his brows together a little, then eased them up as the doubt faded in the face of his unshakable belief in Paul Lightle's cleverness. "He'll have something figured out about that, Constable. Sure as hell."

"Yeah," agreed Cutler dryly. "Sure as hell. When will the wagons be loaded and heading south?"

The fugitive shrugged thick shoulders. "They wasn't sure. It depended on when the mine wagons got up to Gloria, and the bullion was transferred to the war wagons. I figure maybe by yesterday. Maybe today."

Walt tasted the coffee, which was not fresh but which was not undrinkable. He gazed thoughtfully at his prisoner. "John, how long have you been riding with Lightle?"

"A little over two years."

"Smith and Jensen were with him longer?"

"Yeah. About five or six years. There been other fellers, but they got sloughed off for one reason or another. I'll tell you, Constable, they're kind of tight-mouthed, and me—I don't ask a lot of questions."

"Probably a good thing you don't, John. Those other fellers—they got sloughed off for one reason or another. . . . You don't expect Paul, Herman, and Buck, who have been partners so long, would slough you off, do you? You're up here dunging out a livery barn. They're on their way to Mexico, or somewhere, with probably enough gold and silver for the three of them to live like kings for the rest of their lives, and what the hell do they need you for?"

Pinter's reaction was instantaneous. "Not on your lousy life, Constable. I been on raids with them before. We brought things off by workin' like a team. That's what Paul says—each of us knows what to do, an' he does it. We don't make no mistakes. I got an idea you're saying that to make me sweat."

Walt finished his coffee and stood up. "You're going to sweat all right, John. One way or another. Get up."

Walt put Pinter in the cell directly opposite the cell occupied by Frank Bellingham, and as he was turning around after locking the door, Frank raised both hands to the bars and said, "What's he in here for, Constable?"

Walt smiled at the older man, avoided answering his question, and went up to the office where he stood admiring the killing-gun. He probably should have asked Jack Pinter–John Alpen more about himself.

He dropped the gun into a lower desk drawer and went over to the cafe. There were a number of other diners along the counter, including Kelly O'Bryon. Elizabeth smiled—and reddened—and went after Walt's meal. Kelly slid along the bench, pushing his plate and cup with him, until he was beside the constable. Then, knife and fork in hand, he said, "All right. Now tell me something, Walt: just where do I get another dayman this time?"

Walt sat a moment in thought before facing the liveryman. "Kelly, do you still have that green wagon you used last summer out at the Bartlett place to fetch me back to town; that light freight rig with green sideboards you used your matched sorrels on?"

O'Bryon, who was eating, stopped. If there was a connection between him finding another hostler and that pair of matched sorrels with the light freight wagon, he could not find it. "Yeah, I still got the wagon. And those big sorrels, I wouldn't part with them for a farm in Ohio . . . Why?"

Walt watched Elizabeth go down the counter, then return. She saw his admiring gaze, reddened again, and this time she winked as she went past. O'Bryon saw her do that and sat with his mouth open, staring after her. Womenfolk nowadays were as bold as brass. Constable Cutler brought Kelly's attention back when he said, "I'm not sure, but I think maybe I might want to rent that outfit and those big sorrels."

O'Bryon looked toward Elizabeth's curtained-off cooking

area and the large lawman beside him. "The pretty little top-buggy with them cherubs painted on it wasn't good enough?"

Walt turned. "It was just fine. But now I might need a wagon."

O'Bryon affected a knowing look. "Sure. Well, yes, you can have the wagon. Them sorrels, though, I don't hardly never let them out unless I'm driving, an' if you and Miz Bartlett are goin' buggy-ridin' in the light freight wagon you wouldn't want me along."

Cutler considered the face of his friend for a long time, then leaned back off the counter. "It's not for Miz Bartlett and me. And you can drive. You'd be right welcome to come along."

Kelly's incomprehension was increasing by the moment but he thought of himself as being in so deep now that if he admitted he had no idea what this conversation was about, he was going to look not just foolish but also ridiculous. He went back to his meal and spoke around mouthfuls. "What do you want the outfit for?"

"Maybe to drive south a ways."

"When?"

"Right after we've finished eating."

Kelly stopped chewing and turned slowly. "Now? Today?"

"Yes."

"Will you tell me just what in the hell this is all about?"

Walt nodded. "Sure. While we're driving along."

He left the cafe, Kelly O'Bryon staring after him, and returned to the jailhouse to turn loose the fighting freighter.

CHAPTER 13
Two Big Sorrels and a Green Wagon

THERE had been a man named Burton around town until early spring, when he had sold his little house and gone out to Nevada to live with his son and daughter-in-law. During the constable's absences from town he had hired Burton to look after the jailhouse and any prisoners who were in it.

Now Walt had to find someone else. He was leaning in the jailhouse door when Pat Flannery threw him a wave from across the road. Flannery disappeared inside the general store, and Walt Cutler sauntered across and was waiting in overhang shade when Pat emerged carrying a brown paper bag. Walt stopped the barman with a question. "Kelly needs another dayman, Pat; you know of anyone?"

Flannery moved away from the center of the plankwalk as he replied. "Nope, I sure don't. What happened to that feller he took on to replace Bellingham?"

"Locked in one of my cells," Walt replied, and watched the expression of surprise spread over the barman's face. He headed off the question he saw forming on Flannery's lips. "I need someone to look in on him and Frank Bellingham for a day or two, Pat. I got to be out of town. There's not much to it. You get their food three times a day from the cafe, make sure the place is locked up at night. . . ."

Flannery shifted the brown sack from one arm to the other one. In the face of the unexpected request, he had forgotten his astonishment about Kelly's new dayman being in jail. "I'd do it in a minute," he told the lawman, "only I got the saloon to run."

Walt nodded. "How about that feller you hire now and then to mind things?"

Flannery's brow creased. He acted uncomfortable. "Yeah, he's around, but I just don't feel right not mindin' the place myself, unless there's an emergency."

"There is an emergency, Pat, and that's about all I can tell you right now. . . . How many times have I stopped brawls at the saloon when there could have been bottles and mirrors busted and maybe some chairs and tables too?"

Flannery shifted the paper bag back to the other arm. He looked very unhappy. "Real emergency, Walt?"

Walt nodded.

"Well—for how long?"

"A day or two. I'd appreciate it, Pat. Just feed them and keep an eye on things. Don't open their cell doors no matter what. I really do appreciate it. The key ring is on a nail in the wall beside the gun rack." Walt slapped Flannery amiably on the shoulder and struck out for the opposite side of the road.

When he entered the harnessworks Fred was straddling a sewing-horse with curved, broad, viselike jaws, sewing a ripped saddleboot. He nodded unsuspectingly. "Town's quiet, Walt. That Warren gent hasn't been around to pester me about my land in a couple of days. Maybe he taken the measles or something."

Walt leaned on the counter watching Fred sew. "Kelly and I are going to take a drive south in that green light dray wagon of his. We wondered if you'd like to go along; get out of the shop for a while, see the country."

Fred was watching Walt's face. He had stopped sewing. "Where are you going? What's the reason for you and Kelly leavin' town with a wagon?"

"There's been a lot of talk about the condition of the south roadbed lately. Stage passengers raising cain about it, freighters threatening to strike out over private range to make a new trail. Have you heard any of that talk?"

Fred had. A lot of people around town had. For a fact the road had chuckholes, erosion gullies like the ridges on a washboard, only higher and deeper. "I've heard some talk,"

Fred conceded, and sat a moment looking at the gun scabbard in the jaws of his sewing-horse. Then he climbed off and said, "Yeah. I'm about as close to bein' caught up as I'll ever be. When do we go?"

"Kelly's harnessing up right now."

Fred thought that over too. Then his face brightened as he thought he had come up with the reason for leaving town so soon. "You want to be back in time for supper. I don't blame you; Miz Bartlett can cook like no one else around town, and just watchin' her move up an' down behind the counter would be worth the price even if she couldn't cook.

Walt watched him lock the door to the shop. They were almost in front of the jailhouse when Walt stopped. "Fred, suppose we see some antelope out there? Wait, I'll fetch a couple of carbines."

The harnessmaker waited. When Walt emerged to hand one of the Winchesters to him, Fred had a cud in his cheek which he methodically chewed as they resumed their hike southward. Around them the town was approaching its lazy time. There was very little business transacted after the hottest part of the day arrived.

The green-sided wagon had been driven up into the runway, Kelly's pride and joy, the big matched sorrels, on the pole. They eyed Fred and Walt with docile interest. There was no sign of Kelly, but someone was making noises in the harness-room as Walt walked back toward the tailgate and shoved the pair of carbines under a bed of straw that was several inches deep on the wagonbed. Kelly emerged, looked surprised at seeing Fred, then grunted a greeting, and went over to stuff a flour sack filled with rolled barley beneath the seat. He was climbing to the seat when he said, "I never liked seein' animals go hungry." He got settled with one boot on the binder-handle until his passengers were up beside him, then he kicked off the brakes and talked to his horses.

They were heading south past the shacks at the lowest end

of town when he said, "Fred, I thought you'd be workin' on that harness I brought up this morning."

Fred leaned over the side to expectorate before replying. Because it always annoyed him when people said something like that, his retort was curt. "You'll get your damned harness. A man's got a right to take a little fresh air now and then."

Kelly O'Bryon was properly chastened and did not mention the harness again. There was a pale, high overcast, the kind that usually preceded rain by a few days. It was accompanied by utter stillness and a kind of humid heat. Walt examined the sky. "It'll make the stockmen happy," he said, without any need to explain what he meant.

Kelly also looked upwards. "Not if it don't rain," he stated, lowering his eyes to the road ahead. "I've seen it act like this without no rain about as often as I've seen it act like this an' it did rain."

Fred chewed, rocked comfortably with the motion of the wagon, and with thoughts on something that had been prominent among his other thoughts lately, suddenly said, "Kelly, you being a bachelor and all, does it ever seem a man might be better off if he had a wife?"

Kelly turned in surprise. "What for?"

"Well, every blessed pair of socks I got has holes in 'em, and I hate sweepin' out my livin' quarters, an' if Elizabeth Bartlett ever got sick, there bein' no other place in town for a man to eat, I'd starve, and most likely so would you—as well as Walt, here."

The liveryman shifted both lines to one hand, dug out his plug and worried off a corner, settled the cud, and looked at Fred Tower with a puzzled expression. "Who'd marry an old goat like you—or me either, for that matter?"

The harnessmaker leaned to spray tobacco juice again before replying. "Well . . . you never know."

"Yes I do. . . . Fred, have you been ridin' down to Gloria

lately on the sly? You sure as hell aren't sparking any woman in Peralta." Kelly drove a hundred yards before speaking again, and now his expression showed disgust. "Are you goin' through a second childhood or something? You're fifteen years older'n I am. Maybe even older. And you never been married. I know that for a fact because you said so yourself. Now all of a sudden you're thinkin' about getting a wife?"

Fred looked down his slightly beaked nose at the shorter, heavier man. "Fifteen years older'n you? Why you 'possum-bellied, scanty-haired, squinty-eyed screwt, I'm no more'n maybe ten years older than you are."

Constable Cutler had been studying the roadway up ahead. He had listened indifferently to his companions; his thoughts were on what Pinter had told him. He could not convince himself anyone as wily as Ralph Warren—or whatever his name was—would be foolish enough to try to get across the Mexico border after stealing a fortune in bullion bars.

Regardless of what Warren had told Pinter, Walt would have bet a year's wages those war wagons were not traveling south. Not entirely because Warren-Lightle would be too wise to head for Mexico with a fortune, and only himself and two other armed men to protect it, but also because the people down at Gloria, and probably the men from that mine down there, would be around to watch the wagons pull out.

Warren would not dare turn southward when those mine executives would be expecting to see him go directly up north to Denver. He had been able to dupe them into letting him haul their bullion, but he'd never be able to explain to them, after they ran him down, which they certainly would do if he struck out for the border with their bullion, why he was traveling south instead of north.

The choices, then, seemed to Constable Cutler to be either east, west, or actually northward toward Denver, at least in that general direction.

He remembered something Warren had said the day he
and his gunguards had hired horses to ride over the countryside. He had wanted to familiarize himself with the territory
and the roadways. Maybe that had been just talk. Walt leaned
and asked Kelly about those men hiring horses. Kelly, already a little testy after his exchange with Fred Tower,
scowled as he replied.

"Yeah, I remember, and they put a lot of miles on them
horses. Brought 'em back tucked up like gutted snowbirds.
Most folks take care of horses; water 'em when they can, let
'em pick a little grass, and stand in the shade for a spell. Not
those gents. I was half of a mind to say something, but I
didn't."

Walt was interested. "Did they say where they rode?"

"No. Just that they wanted to see the country north an'
west of town. Somethin' about seein' how it looked for
stagecoaches."

Fred jettisoned his cud and reset his hat to conform to the
position of the sun. Mentioning Warren was like waving a
red flag to Fred Tower. He eyed O'Bryon a little bleakly. "We
should have let old Bellingham shoot that buzzard, Kelly."

"Yeah. Except that if Bellingham had missed, which he
sure as hell would have done, Warren would have either shot
him or kicked him to death. He's right handy at kicking
things to death."

His statement about Bellingham prompted another
thought. Kelly leaned around to squint at the lawman. "How
is he doing in your jailhouse, Walt?"

Walt was a moment replying. He had been thinking of
something altogether different. "He's coming along. I'd say
he's a lot better. Eats pretty well now."

"You let him have any whiskey?"

"A little. I'm afraid what might happen if I just cut him
off."

The subject of Frank Bellingham attracted Fred's attention too. "Did you get him those new clothes and all?"

Walt nodded. "Even the boots fit."

"Bertha said something about a bath first. . . . "

"I made him do that too," replied the constable. "He looks like a different man."

Kelly, who knew nothing about Bertha's generosity, had to be told. He was leaning with arms on his legs, slack lines held lightly as he listened. Afterwards he made a little clucking sound. "Now there is a real lady," he told his companions. "I always did think highly of Bertha Maloney."

Fred sat erect and impassive, squinting straight ahead.

Kelly warmed to his subject. "Remember last summer how she took in Elizabeth Bartlett and spoon-fed you until you was better, Walt? I don't think they make 'em like Bertha any more. Do you, Fred?"

The harnessmaker said just one word and did not change expression or take his narrowed eyes off the distant roadway when he answered.

"No."

Kelly continued to drive in a forward slouch. Constable Cutler ignored both his companions to make a long, slow study of the land to the southwest of the roadway. The big horses plodded along as though they had no load behind them. In fact, at their age, in their condition, and being as powerful and large as they were, the green wagon with its three passengers was no load.

"Fred?" Kelly slowly straightened up to lean against the backrest of the seat and turn to stare at the harnessmaker.

"What?"

". . . Bertha Maloney?"

Fred got red as a beet beneath his ingrained tan. He did not open his mouth. Walt gestured. "Turn off the road, Kelly. Over to the right."

Kelly obeyed and said nothing until he had his horses lined out, then he scowled. "What's over here?"

But it was Fred Tower who made the obvious objection. "Walt, you can't look at the condition of the damned road when we're not on it." Tower suddenly stopped speaking, snapped his mouth closed, and looked at Constable Cutler with the piercing intensity of an eagle. "Damn you, I think you done it to me again, Walt Cutler. We didn't come down here to look at no holes in the road. And to think I let you make a monkey out of me when you went after them Winchesters you hid under the straw in back."

Kelly sat straight up. "What Winchesters?"

Fred twisted and pointed downward toward the wagonbed with a rigid arm. "He shoved two saddleguns under that straw when you was in the harness-room gettin' that sack of grain for the horses."

Fred Tower's indignation was awesome. Walt avoided the looks he was getting from his companions and made an elaborate study of the southwesterly range country.

Kelly nudged Fred. "Whatever he's up to, he went and dragooned us again. I got a bad feeling about this ride, Fred. You?"

Fred did not answer; he tapped Constable Cutler on the arm. "You're up to something sure as I'm livin' and breathing . . . Walt, you recollect promisin' me you'd never make me ride out with you again as a posseman?"

Walt nodded. He remembered very well. "This isn't a posse," he replied, then started at the beginning, and told them the entire story—mostly as he suspected things to be, not as he knew them to be, because he actually had very little proof about any of it.

CHAPTER 14
A Pretty Good Liar

NEITHER Tower nor O'Bryon looked pleased, nor did they have anything to say as the wagon rocked across grazing land that looked perfectly flat, and which wasn't when it was ridden over in a light wagon.

What helped tip the scale in Constable Cutler's favor was Fred's dislike of the man calling himself Ralph Warren. Kelly's dislike went back to the episode of the dead puppy, then it went forward to Warren and his companions using three of his livery horses too hard.

It was Kelly who finally spoke. "All right. Why are we goin' west?"

"Because I don't believe those men headed for the Mexico line with that bullion. Warren, or Lightle, or whatever his damned name is, worked all this out like a smart man; would he run for Mexico, just him and his pair of gunfighters or whatever they are? I don't think so. That leaves three other directions. My personal idea is that they are coming north, but more than likely a few miles west of Peralta. . . . Kelly, why would they scour the west country an' ride your horses down doing it, unless they really wanted to know that country?"

O'Bryon nodded his head without speaking.

Walt glanced sideways at Fred, whose slightly predatory, tough features were not as unrelenting as they had been, but they were still not showing sweetness and light. Walt said, "He's a good actor, Fred. He fooled Jim McGregor and you."

The harnessmaker put a flinty look upon the constable. "He never fooled me for a damned minute. I didn't like the looks of him and his partners the first time they walked into the shop. His partners looked like gunmen sure as I'm sitting here."

Walt said no more. There was shimmery heat far to the west. It evidently got thicker the farther west it spread because Walt could not see the distant mountains.

But it did not really feel as hot as it seemed to be. Maybe that haze-like overcast was filtering out some of the sun's heat, which was another of autumn's tricks.

O'Bryon fished a large canteen from beneath the seat and passed it around. Everyone drank. A little farther along Fred shoved back his hat, relaxed against the back of the seat, and while looking between the moving ears of the big horses, made a dry remark.

"An' if we come onto them we got two Winchesters and one pistol. Walt, are you sure there's only three of 'em?"

"That is what Pinter said. Three."

Fred was not satisfied. "If he lied, an' if we see those wagons, the wise thing for us to do would be to turn back, make up a mounted posse, and come back . . . Why did you want to use this wagon anyway?"

"Because fugitives from the law watch for mounted men. Usually quite a bunch of them, armed to the gills. In this kind of country, Fred, if they saw a big armed mounted posse they'd fort up in those wagons and we couldn't even get close enough to burn them out. . . . But another wagon, mainly one like this rig that could belong to any of the cowmen around the countryside, might get them interested, but I don't think they'd fort up. I sure don't want them to get back down inside those wagons."

"Sure not," stated Fred, peering ahead from narrowed eyes. "You want to drive right up onto them and challenge them with two carbines an' one six-gun . . . Walt, those'll be real professional outlaws!"

O'Bryon, who had been listening and occasionally nodding his head in agreement with one speaker or the other, sat up a little straighter, yawned, put both lines onto one hand,

and went searching for his plug again. What he found when he removed it from a pocket was a coating of lint as thick as fungus. Kelly looped his lines around the binder-handle and went to work picking off the largest and most noticeable pieces of lint. That is what he was doing when his matched sorrels raised their heads and pointed dead ahead with their ears. O'Bryon missed it because he was occupied, but neither of his companions did; they recognized the sign and stood up to look in all directions. Their eyesight was not as good as the eyesight of the big horses, but it did not have to be in a sun-brightened, vast expanse of open rangeland; they detected movement south of them and another couple of miles west. Fred watched for a moment then grunted. "Cattle." Walt said nothing until he was sure, then shook his head. Despite heat-haze and distance, anyone who knew cattle knew that they did not walk along of their own free will in two separate bunches, all together and maintaining a regular distance between the two bands of what looked to be about five yards.

But distance played tricks, particularly on shimmery autumn days and when the distance was perhaps two miles or more.

O'Bryon stood up and shaded his eyes. He had done more teamstering than both his companions combined. When he spoke, it was with a voice of authority. "Cattle, hell, those are wagons."

Walt sat down but Fred continued to stand, eyes squinted nearly closed. O'Bryon also remained standing for a few moments, then sat down and unwound the lines to steer his team on an angling, northward course. Fred looked down, then up again. He was gauging Kelly's new course, estimating in his mind where the green wagon would intercept those distant, larger wagons. When he sat down he twisted completely and rummaged in the straw for the Winchesters. As he straightened around he held one carbine between his knees and put the other one across Kelly's lap. He said, "These wagon-sides won't stop bullets, Walt."

They had traveled about another half mile before it seemed that they had been seen. The lead war wagon stopped, someone who looked smaller than a child climbed down and walked back to the second rig. Kelly sighed. "Now comes the interestin' part. Do they figure we're ranch-hands headin' back from town, maybe with supplies—or do they figure something else?"

Fred's opinion was bleakly stated. "If I was in their boots I'd figure it was somethin' else. Just to be on the safe side."

They watched the distant, small figure walk back to the forward wagon, climb up, and as the forward wagon moved out again it was followed by the second rig, but now it was clear to the men with the green wagon that they would be under constant surveillance. Walt said, "Put the Winchesters on the floor behind the dashboard." He was obeyed, but O'Bryon had an objection. "That's not goin' to make any difference, Walt. If Warren is on one of those wagons, he'll recognize all three of us."

Walt's reply to Kelly had nothing to do with anyone being recognized. "Pull more northward, Kelly. Those wagons are riding down on their springs, they're loaded. We can get up ahead out of gun-range and cut across in front of them."

Kelly said, "What good is that going to do?" but he put pressure on his right-hand line, very gradually, so that when the sorrels altered course again they did it almost imperceptibly.

Not another word was said for a long while. The men from Peralta were watching the war wagons as intently as they were being watched in return. Fred put forth a suggestion. "Keep out of Winchester range an' keep moving, Kelly. Walt, there's a way you'n me can stop that lead wagon, an' maybe both wagons. They can't see us any better'n we can see them, but directly they'll be able to. Sidle over into the straw with me. They can't see us down in there. Kelly, aim for that thick stand of wheatgrass, drive right through the middle of it. Me'n Walt will drop over the tailgate with the Winchesters. You drive on. Be sure to keep out of gun-range."

O'Bryon put a slow, skeptical look upon his friend. "And—what?"

"And Walt an' me'll shoot their lead horses. With them dead in their harness, those wagons won't move another yard."

Kelly stared, then swung to squint ahead, and back to the harnessmaker. "Not on your damned tintype, Fred Tower. I'm not goin' to sit up here and watch you shoot those horses."

Fred did not meet the liveryman's irate glare. He shifted the responsibility to Constable Cutler. "Walt—you want to stop those wagons or not?"

Walt wanted to stop them. In fact it was imperative that they be stopped, but shooting the leaders to accomplish that purpose would certainly result in exactly what he did not want to happen—it would warn the outlaws that the green wagon, of which they probably were suspicious, posed a threat, and the outlaws would disappear down inside their wagons.

"We got to think of something else," he replied to Fred while concentrating on the wagons far ahead. "We got to get Warren and his gunguards away from the wagons. So far away they couldn't run back and climb down in before we can reach them."

Fred was disgusted. "How do we do that? Those men got a fortune in those wagons. They got to be as leery as a green colt. I doubt like hell if we really was a rancher an' his wagon headin' for home with supplies, that they'd slack off. They got everything to lose if they stop. The only thing those gents have in their favor right now is—time. They dassn't waste it."

Walt scanned the northward country for cover; for anything at all he could utilize to shield himself and his companions if they tried to stop the wagons. There was nothing. Except for that stirrup-high stand of curing wheatgrass, there was no cover, no underbrush, no trees in the right place, not even an erosion gully deep enough or close enough to the route of the war wagons to hide armed men.

Fred broke the long silence with another suggestion. "All right—we don't shoot the horses then. We can try to pick off two of the men. By your calculations, Walt, that'd only leave one. One man'd give up if he had a lick of common sense. We can lie in that tall grass and both shoot at the same time. Knock two of them plumb out of it."

O'Bryon had no objection this time, and if he had, he would not have had much of a chance to explain it. There was a mounted man coming around from the far side of the second wagon, heading directly toward the green wagon and its occupants. O'Bryon was watching him so intently he scarcely heard Walt say, "Hell, I can still see three men on the seats . . . Fred?"

Fred squinted before replying. "Yes, three. The man on the horse makes four. . . . You was sure there was only three of them, Walt."

The constable had no reply to offer. What was beginning to worry him was the possibility that if there was a fourth man with the wagons, there might be five, or six, or maybe even ten. One thing was very clear: if that oncoming horseman knew any of the three occupants of the green wagon, the alarm would go back to the outlaws. Walt discreetly removed his badge. He also strained to make out the rider as Kelly O'Bryon spoke garrulously. "Where did they have that saddle horse tied? He wasn't trailing at the tailgate."

No one answered, because if the saddle horse had been tied on the far side of the second wagon, which was possible, it would not make any difference; what did make a difference was that the horseman was loping directly toward them. When he was still about a hundred yards away Walt gave a grunt of relief. "Mexican," he exclaimed.

They waited until the rider was closer. Then Kelly spat, watched, and quietly said, "Sure enough."

They were safe from recognition, but as the horseman dropped down to a steady walk, the watchers noticed that while he had his reins visible in his left hand, his right hand was behind the saddle-swells in his lap. The watchers said nothing; they knew why the Mexican had his hand hidden from sight—he had a gun in it.

Walt threw the Mexican a casual wave. The swarthy rider, who was short and heavyset, did not wave back.

When he was close enough, Walt sang out. "What are you fellers hauling? Those look like gravel wagons."

The Mexican did not take his eyes off Fred, Walt, and Kelly. He came up to the big sorrels, halted to let the wagon come up to him, then turned in on the driver's side. He looked behind the seat into the wagonbed, then studied each of the seated men separately before he spoke. He had an accent but his English was good enough—it was in fact better than most border-Mexicans spoke. He looked at Walt when he asked who they were and where they were going.

Walt took a fairly safe gamble. He did not believe the Mexican was familiar with the countryside. "Heading back to the ranch," he told the dark, wary man with the gun in his lap. "We been to Peralta for the mail and some medicine for the old gent we work for." Walt gestured. "We're about halfway home." He dropped the arm. "Are you fellers hauling rock?"

The Mexican shook his head, seemed to reconsider, and spoke as he made a crooked little smile. "Not exactly rock like you put on roads. We are hauling ore samples."

Walt looked as though he believed that. "You've got a long way to go before you find a town with an assay office in it," he told the horseman. "You got lots of miles to cover, friend."

The Mexican nodded, raised his hat, scratched, and put the hat back on. It was clearly a signal. The men on the wagon seat recognized it as such. The Mexican spoke again, sounding less wary. "This ranch where you work—where is it?"

Walt made another careless gesture. "Northwest, the way we're going. Maybe six, eight miles from where we are now."

For a while the mounted man said nothing as he continued to examine the men and their wagon. In the end he looked admiringly at the matched sorrels, and finally, as he was lifting his reins, he said, "Them horses is worth a lot of money. Where I come from you could get a lot of land for them."

O'Bryon nodded and the Mexican nodded back and turned his horse. He rode back the same way he had arrived, at a comfortable lope.

Kelly leaned to look around Fred at Constable Cutler. "You're a pretty good liar, for a man who ain't supposed to." He talked up the team and held them to the same course they had been traveling.

Over at the big wagons four men were on the ground palavering. The Mexican was recognizable because he was holding the reins to his horse as he waved in the direction of the green wagon.

Fred shook his head. He had sweated bullets during the previous meeting. What bothered him most was not having his shellbelt and six-gun.

Walt leaned forward watching the palavering men across the middle distance. While he was watching, another man climbed down over the side of the foremost war wagon. "Five of them," he murmured.

Fred frowned. "Five that we can see. If there's supposed to be only three, and that turns into five, there darned well could be more inside those wagons."

O'Bryon watched the meeting up ahead break up as men went to the wagons, climbed up, and he clearly heard the whistle when the leading wagon got under way again. This close, on a paralleling course, Kelly had an opportunity to study the hitches and the rigs.

There were four horses on each wagon. Somewhere on the far side of the second wagon, there was a lead horse. He straightened back on the seat as he said, "Good animals. Big, stout ones an' they don't look like they've missed many meals. And them wagons is heavy as hell. Loaded, they make those horses dig in for each step."

Walt straightened up slowly. He was beginning to form an idea. "Drive right past and keep on driving," he told Kelly.

O'Bryon was perfectly willing. He had not cherished the prospect of a gunfight way out here in the middle of nowhere without any other shelter than his green wagon—and with a carbine with just one set of bullets in its slide.

CHAPTER 15
A Long Drive

FRED TOWER put a quizzical look on the lawman. "Nightfall?" he said.

Walt nodded. "Nightfall. They can't go any faster than they are goin' right now. At that pace they're still goin' to be out here in open country come dusk. They can't push those horses, not if they expect to get very far. Kelly, you know wagons. How much weight would you figure those horses are pulling?"

O'Bryon wagged his head. He had no intention of making a guess that would turn out incorrect and giving either of his companions the opportunity to remind him of an error for the rest of his life.

"A lot," he replied to Walt. "A hell of a lot of weight. How much gold and silver is supposed to be in them rigs?"

Walt looked at Kelly with a rueful expression. "A lot. I'm not sure even Jim McGregor would know."

The day was wearing along. Even so, at this time of year, daylight lingered an hour of two after sunset. Kelly squinted northwestward, the course he had set for his big sorrel horses. His private estimate was that they would pass in front of the war wagons with perhaps as much as a mile separating them, which was good enough for gun-range. But by the time it was dark enough for the outlaws to lose sight of the green wagon, they were going to be several miles farther than he thought they should be if Walt's intention was to stop and sneak back on foot toward the outlaw-camp.

He spat, shifted a little on the hard seat, studied the laden rigs, and finally said, "We're goin' to have a long walk tonight, Walt."

Walt had already made his estimate and nodded his head. Nothing more was said until they were in front of the oncoming war wagons, then Fred turned to look southward and wag his head. "Constable," he said a little formally, "this time I think you bit off a pretty big bite."

Walt did not offer a contradiction. The same thing that was worrying the harnessmaker was worrying him. There were five heavily armed outlaws with those wagons, not three. Something else passed through his mind too. Suppose Ralph Warren was legitimately transporting that bullion? Suppose he had not lied to the mine company's executives? He most certainly was heading in the general direction of Denver. That Jack Pinter would have lied to him Walt did not doubt.

As for Ralph Warren having five men with his wagons instead of just himself and his two gunguards, that could be very rationally explained: a large load of ingots was rarely if ever transported without plenty of armed men acting as an escort.

Walt Cutler turned to watch the laden wagons but Kelly only glanced southward. His interest was in crossing in front of them and continuing to tool his rig on its westering course.

It was the harnessmaker who finally broke the long silence. "You made a lucky guess, Walt, figuring those wagons would be out here heading north." He paused long enough to make another appraisal of the large wagons, then also said, "Since we got a lot of time before we sneak up on those gents, tell me something: if you'd known there was five men with them rigs, would you have got up a decent posse to come after them?"

Walt thought he probably would have. "Maybe, Fred, but I know how they would have reacted to a mounted posse coming out here."

The harnessmaker thought for a while, then curled his lips in a sardonic grin. "Yeah. They'd have ducked down inside their wagons and shot through the loopholes, an' it came to me just now that's what it must have been like when the broncos attacked settler wagons, them inside, the redskins outside ridin' round and round." He nudged Kelly O'Bryon. "If we was with a posse, Kelly, this time we'd be the Indians."

O'Bryon put a pained look on his friend. He was not in the mood for speculation, even ones that were supposed to be ironically amusing.

They continued to travel on their established course. The men with the laden wagons watched them from their high seats without seeming to be very concerned. Evidently the impression the men with the green wagon had made on the *vaquero* had been convincing.

It had been, but neither Walt, Fred, nor Kelly knew why. What the Mexican had ridden back to report was that two of the strangers with the light wagon were old, and the third one was younger, but of the three, only the younger man was wearing a sidearm. Three men with only one gun between them were not likely to be much of a threat.

The day was fading, and the heat which had made a blue blur of distances was lessening. That veil-like high overcast had begun to dissipate. By moonrise the sky would be as clear as it usually was.

Kelly was hungry and complained that if Walt had known they were going to be way to hell and gone out in the grassland, the least he could have done was fetch along a sack of vittles.

Fred considered the meaty teamster. "You could do like they tell me camels do, Kelly. You could live off your hump for a month."

O'Bryon got a fresh cud into his cheek, ignored his companions, and watched the rumps of his big horses. With daylight beginning to acquire the faint sootiness of oncoming dusk, Kelly seemed to forget his hunger. He chewed, expectorated, and rode along loosely and relaxed. When Walt looked back, Kelly said, "I been figuring, Walt . . . if we stop those wagons and maybe, somehow or other, come out of this alive, how much reward do you expect that mining company would give to get their bullion back?"

Before Walt answered, the harnessmaker stared at O'Bryon. This idea had not once occurred to him, but now as he dwelt upon it, the better he liked it. "Ought to be worth maybe as much as a thousand dollars for each of us, wouldn't you say, Walt?"

Constable Cutler squared around on the seat, scanned the faintly sooty sky, and reflected briefly on the perfidy of human nature before answering. "You two have been riding along mad at me and worried about the odds against us out here—right up until you came up with this notion. Does that money make that much difference?"

O'Bryon answered instantly. "Sure," he said.

The harnessmaker put it more pragmatically. "Constable, you got us out here, an' you got us up to our butts in real serious trouble if we try to catch those men and take over their wagons. Now don't you figure we got a right to have a decent inducement to risk our necks?"

Walt grinned. "Yeah, I guess so." He regarded his old friends. One thing he knew about them from having been through an earlier, very bad episode with them was that while they grumbled a lot and swore and complained, they would not take a backward step. "I'll put in for a thousand for each of you when we get back."

Fred sighed. "If we get back." He groaned aloud. "Right this minute I'd trade new money for my shellbelt and six-gun."

Walt looked over his shoulder. The war wagons were passing over the green wagon's tire tracks bearing steadily northward. He watched for a long while, then squared around wearing a scowl. "I got an idea," he muttered, and Fred looked down his nose at the lawman as he murmured, "Be kind to it, son; it's in a mighty strange place."

As though he had not heard the disparaging remark, Walt turned his head to the right to study as much of the north-ward area as he could make out in the diminishing daylight. "They've already scouted up this country," he said, not speaking to anyone in particular. "My idea is that the reason they did that was so they'd know where to make their camp when they got up here with the war wagons."

O'Bryon settled against the back of the seat. "You think that's a new idea? What other reason would they have for riding my horses so hard?"

Walt's reply was short. "All right. They know where to camp. But we know this country a lot better than they do. Where would you camp, Kelly?"

He asked this of O'Bryon because, as a teamster, his answer would have taken into consideration the essentials any teamster would naturally consider necessary: grass and water.

For a while the green wagon moved along, tailgate-chain rattling, sideboards grinding in their brackets over uneven ground, the sorrel horses nearly as fresh now as they had been three hours earlier. Then the liveryman straightened up. "Hell, you know where they're goin' to fetch up if they don't change course? If they scouted up the countryside they got to know the only water up this close to the neck is that sidehill spring a mile or less from the ashes of the Bartlett house." Kelly looked past Fred at the constable. "They can pick up the ruts and follow them right into the neck, cross to the slope, and make camp at the base of the hill where that spring is. You know—that spring where Elizabeth Bartlett knocked the rangeman off his horse with a rock in the head?"

Fred looked disapprovingly at the liveryman. "What do you mean—does he know? Walt lay out there after that rangemen shot him an' left him for dead. A man don't forget a place like that."

Walt headed off an argument by saying, "Turn north, Kelly. Head for the neck. They can't see us now any more than we can see them."

But hard-headed Fred Tower had an observation to make. "If we don't angle a hell of a distance more west, Walt, they won't have to see us, all they got to do is stop and listen."

That was true. As still as this evening was, as clear as the air was, and with that tailgate-chain rattling, along with the other sounds an unladen wagon would make, the men with the laden wagons would hear Kelly's rig paralleling them, and that would undo the convincing act Fred, Walt, and Kelly had put on the *vaquero*.

O'Bryon drove a short distance, then hauled down to a halt, and looked around Fred at the constable. "He's right."

Walt did not dispute it; he swung to the ground. "Climb down and bring the carbines . . . Kelly, do your big horses carry double?"

O'Bryon was leaning to pick up one of the Winchesters. He hesitated, then grasped the weapon, and nodded his head as he twisted to climb down on the near side. "Yeah. They're broke to ride or drive." Kelly stood beside his wagon until Fred was also on the ground, Winchester in hand. "All right. They won't hear us ridin' up there, but if this turns into a horse race, we're goin' to lose."

Taking the sorrels off the wagon-tongue and dumping their harness into the wagonbed did not take long. Climbing onto the broad backs of the sorrels did, though. Fred stepped onto a wheel hub and sprang across a horse's back holding the Winchester in his right hand, the short rein in his left hand. Kelly had a more difficult time mounting. For one thing his legs were shorter. For another thing his paunch got in the way for jumping, so he had Fred ride up close to a sideboard, balanced there until all he had to do was swing his leg over, and he got astride behind Fred Tower.

Walt vaulted across the back of the second sorrel. Both horses stood perfectly still until they had riders on their backs, then turned their heads as far as they could, which was not far enough because blinders limited their view. They were surprised and uncertain. They were indeed combination horses, and in their lives they had pulled a lot of things but had not carried very many. What made it possible to rein them out was their very tractable dispositions. They did not appear to object to having men on their backs but were not sure what was going to be expected of them.

As they left the wagon behind in the deepening gloom of late dusk, Kelly groaned. His big sorrel horses had very wide backs, so much wider than a saddle animal that he felt like he was being pulled apart.

Fred had no trouble: Fred was not only lean and long-legged, but he had been at home on a horse's back since he had been a very small child.

Walt led the way. Occasionally he halted to listen. Sound carried but even so the laden wagons did not make a lot of it so they had to halt more often than perhaps they normally would have, until Walt was satisfied that the outlaws and their stolen bullion had reached the faint ruts leading into the neck of land where Elizabeth Bartlett and her husband had staked out their homestead, and where she had lived until her husband had died the year before.

There was nothing up there now but ash from the cabin and a sagging woodshed. The neck of land appeared in weak starlight as a wide meadow with low, cut-over hills to the north and south. The grass was rank because there had been no livestock grazing over it, and also because this year there had been a wet spring.

Walt rode with haunting memories of this place. He no longer had to halt to listen; he had freshly crushed grass in wide ruts to guide him. When he came abreast of the black char where the cabin had been, he thought of Elizabeth's late husband who had died in there, his wasted body consumed by the fire which had burned the rough little homesteader's house to the ground.

This was where he had first seen Elizabeth. She had looked very different from how she looked now. The anguish, exhaustion, and terrible ordeal she had lived through watching her husband die by inches were gone now, after a year. Bertha Maloney was right: It had taken at least a year.

Fred cleared his throat. He had spoken, and Walt had not heard him. This time he also raised his arm to point in the direction of the sidehill spring with its stirrup-high grass and tangled underbrush. "I think they stopped," he said, and lowered his arm.

The big sorrel horses stood motionless until their riders were satisfied that, indeed, there was no longer any sound of heavy wagons up ahead.

Fred did not wait for the constable's decision; he slid to the ground gripping his saddlegun. Kelly came down too, but with considerably less grace, and he flexed his knees several times to make certain they would work properly. It had been a very long time since Kelly had ridden a horse—an even longer time since he had ridden one bareback.

Dusk had deepened into night. There was starlight but as yet no moon. When it eventually arrived, it would be fuller than it had been the previous few nights, and that could be both an advantage and a disadvantage.

As Kelly led his horses away to be cared for, the harness-maker eyed Constable Cutler. "Those gents are goin' to be as spooked as they can be. Might not be more than a couple of 'em sleep at a time tonight. I know if I was in their boots I wouldn't sleep without havin' a hell of a heavy guard out . . . Sneaking up onto them ain't going to be easy."

Walt waited until Kelly returned, then said, "We're not going to sneak up on the men. We're going to find their horses and chouse them out of the country."

CHAPTER 16
The Sickle Moon

FRED TOWER, who had once been a trail-drover and who knew quite a bit about sneaking up on hobbled horses, or loose ones for that matter, was of the opinion that if all three of them scouted up in the direction of the spring where the outlaws were establishing their camp, the chances of being discovered would be much greater than if one man did it.

He was right, so Walt and Kelly waited until he was out of sight, then got comfortable on the ground with their backs to the haunting wreckage of the burned-out homesteader's shack. Kelly, who was not by nature a prudent individual, seemed to sense that Constable Cutler did not want to talk about what had happened in this place the previous year.

Kelly was also superstitious, something very few people knew, so occasionally he glanced uneasily over his shoulder in the direction of the mound of char and ash where Elizabeth's husband had perished.

Walt Cutler was concentrating on the outlaws, the war wagons, and Fred Tower up there somewhere in darkness in an area where Walt was certain he would be shot on sight if the outlaws saw him. Unlike Kelly O'Bryon, he did not allow his thoughts to go back to his earlier encounter in this place.

A wolf howled over through the timber and underbrush on the north hillside, and Kelly started where he sat. Walt glanced to his left; wolves ordinarily did not come anywhere near where there was a scent of men, and because they had a very keen sense of smell, it seemed improbable that this particular lobo had not picked up such a scent down in the neck. Walt guessed that this wolf was an old gummer, reduced to scavenging, perhaps with dulled senses and a wandering mind.

Kelly said, "What's that darned thing doing here?"

Walt shrugged and strained to hear noise from up near the spring. There was a little noise, the kind it was unavoidable to make when men with wagons and eight harness-horses were setting up a camp by feeble starlight.

Kelly watched the north slope and muttered under his breath. Of all the areas in the Peralta countryside he would prefer not to be, this was foremost. He groped for his tobacco plug and said, "That damned wolf isn't too far from where I put out my horses."

Walt turned. In the ghostly light he could easily read the liveryman's expression. "He won't bother your horses, Kelly. Most likely he's a half-blind old dog-wolf stove up with rheumatism looking for mice."

The liveryman chewed, spat, and faced in the direction of the spring only when a man's loud laughter came down through the night.

It was a long wait before Fred returned, coming up to them from the south, badly startling Kelly by soundlessly appearing and dropping down with a grunt as he said, "They got a lantern. I counted five of 'em. Two took the horses out to hobble them in the grass, then went back where the others was making up a meal."

Walt said, "No fire?"

Fred shook his head. "Maybe they figure it'd be too risky, but hell, no one could see a fire from where they are, unless they was down here." He got comfortable on the ground. "We better give 'em a couple of hours."

"Did you see the horses?"

"Yeah. From the sound I'd say they got chain hobbles. I wasn't close enough to make out whether they was the army kind. If they are, all we got to do is unbuckle 'em." Fred paused to pull a stalk of grass and chew it. "If it's those chain hobbles with steel anklets and a padlock, why then I expect we'll have to think of something else." He spat out the grass stalk. "I haven't seen anyone use real chain hobbles in years, not since the army rounded up all the Indians an' took them away. Using chain hobbles on your horses was about the only way you could go to sleep at night an' be sure they would be around come daylight. But chains chafed a horse's fetlocks. People quit using them some years back." Fred gazed at Kelly. "What's bothering you?"

Walt gestured. "There's a wolf over on the north slope. Kelly's worried about his horses."

Fred dismissed this as too unimportant even to comment about and returend to his former topic. "I got a fair look at those wagons. I think they got belly-dumps; the kind folks use to spread gravel and manure and whatnot while they're driving along."

Walt was interested. He had seen his share of war wagons. This was the first time he had heard of any that opened from the bottom like manure spreaders.

Fred searched for another grass stalk. "Maybe the wagons were originally dump-rigs, and somebody doubled their sides and reinforced them with steel and made war wagons out of them." He finally selected a stalk that appealed to him, pulled it loose, and chewed on it as he sprawled on the ground. "Walt, we got all night. Maybe what we'd ought to do is one of us go back to town and round up some possemen."

Kelly, who had been silent for a long time, nodded his head in approval of this idea but said nothing.

Walt's answer indicated that he had already considered this. "Won't be any need, Fred, if we can run their horses off. They won't go anywhere without animals to pull their wagons, and I doubt that they'll want to abandon them . . . After we chouse off their teams, then we can go back and make up a posse, but first I want to make damned sure they aren't going to be somewhere else come daylight."

The harnessmaker chewed grass, pondered for a while, then grunted agreement as he lowered himself flat out in the grass, pushed his hat down over his face and said, "Kelly, wake me when it's time to go back up there."

O'Bryon did not say a word. He watched the harnessmaker clasp both hands over his stomach and go to sleep. It annoyed hell out of him that Fred could do that when there was a confounded lobo wolf on the upper sidehill of that north slope, and behind them was what remained of a shack a dead man had been burned to cinders in, and whose troubled spirit was probably right this damned minute hovering somewhere close by, loaded down with all kinds of anguish, miseries, and harrowing sadness.

The constable also lay back but he did not close his eyes. Kelly got to his feet to go look at his sorrel horses. As he passed the rear of the burned little house he did not turn his head. Wild horses could not have made him turn his head.

Fred lifted his hat, looked around, then spoke to Walt. "What's bothering him?"

Walt's answer was brusque. "Ghosts. He almost jumped out of his britches when that old wolf sounded."

Fred eased back down and replaced his hat so that when he spoke again it sounded like he was down in a well. "Walt? I keep comin' back to something."

Walt looked over, guessed what it was, and lay back gazing straight up again. "You're making a mountain out of a molehill."

The harnessmaker lifted the hat to peer across the distance between them. "I haven't told you what I got on my mind."

"I know. You don't have to tell me."

"What is it, then?"

"Bertha."

Fred Tower continued to gaze across the little distance for a moment before easing back down with the hat over his face. "How is that a mountain out of a molehill?"

"If you didn't misunderstand her; if she really is interested in you, you're lucky, Fred."

"It's not exactly that, Walt. It's being married."

Walt waited before answering because he thought he heard horses moving up near the sidehill spring. But the noise, whatever it had been, stopped. "I've never been married, Fred, but I came awfully close one time, and I have a notion I'll really do it directly now—so I guess I'm not the best person you could talk about marriage with. But if you want one man's personal opinion, I think you and Bertha would make a real good team . . . And what would you be losing? Nothing. You'd still have the harnessworks; she'd still have her rooming house."

"They get bossy."

Walt had to think about that. It was possible that Bertha might get bossy. She was certainly an individual of strong ideas. Before he could frame a reply Kelly O'Bryon came back, sank down between them with a groan, and said he was hungry as hell. This interlude pretty well finished off Fred's anxieties and Constable Cutler's advice about them.

They were all hungry. They were also going to be cold before daylight returned. None of them had come out here prepared to spend the night. Fred lifted his hat, gazed at O'Bryon from an impassive face, and rolled up to his feet thinking privately that he would rather go scout up the outlaw camp again than lie there waiting for the cold to make his joints stiff while Kelly O'Bryon complained.

Walt sat up to watch Fred walk away. He looked for the moon and found it, curved thickly upwards from the bottom. An errant thought occurred to him. The stockmen did not like this kind of a moon. If a powderhorn could be hung from a sickle moon and would not slide off, it was going to rain. This particular moon was too low at the bottom of the curve for a powderhorn not to slide off, which signified a dry spell.

Walt shrugged that off as he watched Fred fade out in the darkness and wondered if he and Kelly should not have gone with him. But this time the wait was shorter. When

Tower returned he said the camp lantern had been extinguished, and he had been able to creep closer. There were several lumpy bedrolls beside the wagons. There was a sentry sitting on one of the high wagon seats cradling a long-barreled rifle in his arm. Normally men armed with carbines did not like the idea of an adversary having the greater range a rifle provided, but as Walt go to his feet he reflected that in darkness it did not matter how far a man could shoot, it mattered how accurately he could shoot.

Fred rapped Kelly's boot soles. The liveryman sat up rubbing his eyes. He had fallen asleep in spite of himself. He asked the harnessmaker if it was not too early for them to safely chouse the horses, and Fred shook his head when he replied. "It won't get any better if we wait."

As Kelly arose he winced. Straddling the broad-backed horse had made him sore, and the creeping chill of night had not helped that any.

Fred led the way. Kelly had difficulty walking until he had covered about half the distance to the uphill spring, then his problems vanished, and he slipped up beside Walt. Both of them strained to see the wagons and the camp, but Fred was leading them on a northwesterly course, in the direction of some large trees, tall and bristly in the pale moonlight. Beyond the trees, dark shapes of hobbled horses were discernible against the backgrounding slope, which went directly upwards in the vicinity of the spring.

Fred halted, leaned on his carbine, and studied the animals. Two of them had caught movement and were now facing in the direction of the motionless men. The other horses were farther off and had seen nothing. They were cropping grass and because feed was abundant up here, they did not have to hop very often.

Walt counted. He came up with eight horses and looked inquiringly at the harnessmaker. There should have been nine horses. He said the saddle horse was missing, and Fred nodded about that. "I think he's on the far side of the wagons but I couldn't get over there to make sure. Walt, if we can stampede these horses, that saddle horse isn't going to help them much."

Walt wagged his head. "All they need to round up the harness-horses is one saddle horse, Fred. We want to put them completely afoot."

Tower hoisted his carbine as he replied, "Wait here. I'll see if I can duck around the rear of the wagons without that feller on the wagon seat seeing me. If there is a horse over there I'll try to lead it back."

Fred eased away with Walt's troubled gaze on him. If Fred found the saddle horse and tried to lead it away, that sentry was going to hear, provided he was not asleep. It was so utterly still where the outlaw camp was that even a man's breathing would be audible for a surprising distance.

Kelly sank to one knee, resting on his upright Winchester. When Walt spoke, the liveryman gave a little start.

"We better go back through the trees where we can keep an eye on that sentry."

They had not gone far before one of the harness-horses they were leaving behind raised its head and loudly whinnied. From a considerable distance he got back an answer, and as Walt came out of the trees he could see the man on the high wagon seat standing up and looking southward, down in the direction of the burned-out cabin.

He wanted to swear. One of Kelly's big sorrels had replied to the horse that had whinnied. The sentry was alerted. Perhaps he would think there was a loose ranch horse back down there. But then again, he might think the sorrel's answer had been made by a ridden horse, perhaps one of a number of ridden horses belonging to manhunters.

Walt watched the man. He was short and thick, possibly that *vaquero* they had met earlier. The longer he stood there looking southward, evidently waiting for another horse call or possibly for sounds of mounted men approaching, the more time it gave Fred.

The sentry seemed agitated for a few minutes; then apparently satisfied that it had been a loose horse, he settled down. In a little while he was relieved of guard duty by a tall, gangling man.

Walt was almost certain that the new man was Herman Smith, the one Fred Tower had argued with in his harness shop.

CHAPTER 17
Too Easy—Too Bad

THE easy-moving outlaw stood beside the first wagon briefly looking around, taking the measure of the night, then returned to his sleeping area, picked up another of those long-barreled rifles, shrugged into a blanket-lined old riding coat, and went over to start climbing toward the wagon seat.

Kelly nudged Walt and gestured. They could catch the relief sentry while he was spread-eagled against the side of the wagon. Walt shook his head; if they tried that they would be in among the outlaws, one squawk from the relief sentry, and all hell would break loose, with them in the middle of it.

Kelly watched the sentry complete his climb and get comfortable up there where he had a good view in all directions—except that with less than a half moon and a rash of stars which supplied even less light, visibility was drastically limited. More than seeing in the night, though, it was the sentry's duty to listen, and the man seemed to be doing this.

Fred Tower came up behind them without a sound and whispered, "I got the saddle horse."

Walt stiffened, and Kelly gave a controlled start. They turned.

Fred grinned at them and said softly, "Led him west a fair distance, then set him loose. Last I saw, he was followin' down some scent heading toward the flat ground. Maybe he picked up the smell of Kelly's sorrels."

Walt nodded. "We thought we heard you, but the guard up there didn't."

Fred's professional ability was wounded by that remark. The smile vanished, and his voice sank to a growl when he said, "Only way you heard me was if you got ears like an elephant. That horse never made a sound." Fred touched his chest where an old jacket had been when he had left them earlier. "I tied rags around all his four feet. Thank the Lord he wasn't fidgety. And somebody owes me for a new jacket."

Walt gazed at the harnessmaker with increasing respect. "You surprise me every now and then," he murmured, and perhaps because Fred Tower thought this might lead into a lot of questions about how he knew these horsethief tricks, he pointed to the man on the wagon seat. "We don't have forever. It's gettin' cold, which means the night is movin' along. What do you want to do about old eagle-eye up there? If we wait around a few more hours until the light gets better he's goin' to see us, and there aren't too many places to hide up here."

Walt jerked his head, starting back the way they had come through the unkempt large old trees in the direction of the hobbled harness horses. He was not very concerned with the sentry on his wagon seat. For one thing those big old trees barred the view from the camp to the grassy place where the horses were. For another thing, once the eight team animals were run off, the sentry was not going to have to see Fred, Walt, and Kelly to know there was someone out there in the night. Those departing big horses would make enough noise to wake the dead.

The men split up, each one heading for a different horse. What Fred had feared—that the hobbles would be of that old-fashioned kind with steel anklets and padlocks—proved not to be the case. The horses had been hobbled with the most common variety of hobbles; leather cuffs with large buckles which encircled each pastern and were connected between the two cuffs with several links of chain bound in the middle by a steel swivel. They were the easiest kind of hobbles to use, and they were the easiest kind to remove. As Walt finished with his first animal and dropped the hobbles in the grass, the horse watched him owlishly as he moved toward another horse.

When all eight team horses were free, they milled, nervously picked a little grass, raised their heads occasionally to look around. They knew they were free. What troubled them was that they were not being led somewhere after the hobbles had been removed.

A large seal-brown gelding with a Roman nose stood motionless for a long time, probably trying to comprehend something in his small brain that was unprecedented in his experience and therefore incomprehensible to him. But he knew two things: he was free of hobbles, and he was in open country. He did not run, he simply began walking southward, down the gradual long slope. He did not look left or right, he ignored the other horses, but as they watched him, they followed.

Walt, standing with his companions, listened when Kelly said, "I'd have bet good money that when they found out they was loose, they'd go busting down out of here like the devil was behind them."

Walt nodded. So did Fred. What the team horses were doing was certainly not unheard of, but it was rare. Ordinarily, freed horses celebrated their freedom by running, maybe bucking and snorting as they went, but running one way or another.

Fred said, "Tired. They been used hard lately. Those wagons are heavy."

But that wasn't it, and Fred probably did not really believe what he said himself; he had just felt impelled to say something. Walt led the way back through the trees until they could see the camp and the sentry. The man was sitting up there holding the rifle between his knees with his head slightly cocked to one side. He was listening to something, but he did not seem very greatly alarmed by whatever it was.

Walt elected not to press their luck any further. He jerked his head to lead the way back over beyond the trees where they could start back down toward the cabin rubble and be invisible in the darkness.

Somewhere ahead the team horses were wandering, moving apart from one another. Walt could occasionally hear one of them, but with rank grass underfoot unless their shod hooves struck rock, they would not make any noise.

Walt stopped to look back. As he did this Kelly spoke. "I think he heard the horses. The way he was sittin' and all."

Fred made one of his eminently practical observations. "Partner, you can bet your life that if he figured that was their teams leavin' the country he'd have rousted out his friends and by now all hell would be busting loose."

Walt lengthened his stride. Originally, he had planned to stampede the horses once they were free to run, and he had been very much aware that stampeding horses would have awakened the outlaws and there would have been pursuit, and not just of the horses either.

He was at a loss to understand why the horses had simply walked away the way they had done, but he was enormously relieved that they had. By the time he and his companions were back down to level ground, Walt was elated that the harness animals were gone, and he, Fred, and Kelly had achieved their objective. They had stranded five renegades up a sidehill with bullion-laden wagons they could not possibly move without horses—and the horses were gone.

Kelly was so pleased with their success he slapped Fred on the back, and even Fred with his somewhat skeptical and dour disposition smiled broadly as they went in the direction of O'Bryon's big sorrels. All they had to do now was return to Peralta, round up a posse, and come back armed to the teeth, and if Ralph Warren wanted to make a fight out of it, they'd give him all the fighting he wanted.

Kelly's big horses had company. Three of the freed animals from up by the spring were out there with them, getting acquainted and acting as docile as kittens when the three two-legged creatures emerged out of darkness. One of Kelly's sorrels nickered softly. Kelly responded by walking over to scratch the horse's neck before searching in the grass for the bridles he had dropped out there.

Walt looked over his shoulder. He was finally beginning to feel uneasy; their objective had been achieved too easily.

Fred said, "Wait until I'm up there, Kelly," and vaulted astride one of the large horses, then leaned with an extended arm to assist Kelly to mount behind him.

It didn't work because Fred had nothing to grip with his free hand and Kelly's weight almost pulled Fred off. So Walt walked over, got positioned with one knee bent for Kelly to step onto, then boosted the liveryman into position.

As Walt was walking over to the second large sorrel horse, a man's cry of alarm shattered the night-long hush. Moments later there were other shouts. Walt paused briefly to listen, then sprang across his big horse, reined around, and led the withdrawal from the neck. Fred followed, but first got behind those three freed horses and drove them ahead as though they were sheep. That was how they traveled too, docile even when they were being boosted over into an ungainly gallop.

Walt sat twisted looking back. The commotion a mile away up the slope was less noisy now but someone had lighted the camp lantern and was bobbing around with it over where the hobbled horses had been. "Found the hobbles in the grass," he called to Fred and Kelly, and faced forward to keep his big horse in a lope. Riding a twelve-hundred-pound, pudding-footed harness-horse in any gait but a walk was jarring because large horses went up awkwardly and came down awkwardly. Even if they were accustomed to galloping, which they were not, they were simply too large and massive to be comfortable to ride. Being bareback emphasized this, but none of the men from Peralta said a word. Behind them were some furious outlaws, two of whom, Buck Jensen and Herman Smith, had impressed even Kelly O'Bryon as gunmen and killers.

Walt left the ruts on a southerly course before reaching the open country beyond the neck. He pushed his big horse up the stump-littered sidehill, which was not very high, and pushed him down the far side, in this way cutting about a half-mile off the route toward Peralta.

At the base of the hill he turned eastward and slightly

southward, which was the direction to Peralta. The low hill they had just crossed ran along the south side of the neck of Bartlett land for more than a mile, and over across it nearly a mile eastward was the location of that spring where the outlaws had camped, which meant that as they fled toward town, the three bareback riders did not even parallel their enemies for a quarter of an hour, by which time it was necessary to slacken their gait. O'Bryon's big sorrels were not saddle horses; they had never been conditioned to withstand running; they had been raised and trained to pull, not run.

Walt watched the low ridge on his left as they rode out a short distance from its base. There was no noise, or, if there was, it could not be detected at that distance and with the thick hill to muffle it.

Fred said, "They're sure as hell goin' to catch some of those horses, as tame as they are." He jutted his chin in the direction of the three horses he was still driving along. "Not countin' these they'd still have five—if they catch them. That's enough to move one wagon."

Walt nodded. This was the first flaw in his plan. The harness-horses had been too tame and docile, which was why they had not stampeded. If they had been a little less tame they would have run like the wind. Also, if they had run like the wind, the outlaws would have come boiling out like hornets. This way, Walt and his friends had run almost no risk in escaping. But there was extreme risk now of their being caught if those outlaws were given enough time to catch some of their freed horses. In fact, all it would take to move one wagon was four rounded-up horses.

Walt studied the sky. Dawn was coming but it would be a while yet in arriving. He glanced to his left, against the south side of that low barrier hill that protected the Bartlett homestead from winter winds. He did not see anything.

CHAPTER 18
On the Trail to Peralta

WALT boosted his large team animal over into his uncollected and hard-riding gallop again. Up ahead, where a spit of timber came down upon the flat land, there was a possibility that the fleeing men could reach protective shelter. At least if they could get among those big old trees, anyone looking for them with a long-range Winchester rifle would have a hell of a time seeing them.

But Walt did not head for the spit of trees, he angled away from them in a beeline for town. He and his companions were out of rifle range, but the big sorrels were making noises like leaky bellows, so they were hauled down to a steady walk with their riders looking back.

There was no sign yet of anyone following them. But Fred punched a cud into his cheek, spat, and watched their back trail like a hawk.

The moon was leaving, the stars were less bright, and a pastel shade of dark blue seemed to be taking over the heavens, which had previously been fully dark blue, or dark black.

Walt guessed that if they alternated between loping and walking, they might be able to reach town an hour or so after sunrise. It was not an altogether reassuring thought, now that the possibility of the outlaws being able to move their bullion, at least part of it, seemed entirely possible. His bleak thoughts were interrupted by Fred Tower.

"I think we can set these team horses loose now, Walt."

Cutler nodded. Even if the outlaws found those three horses, caught them, and returned to the spring with them, by the time they had them on a wagon-tongue ready to pull,

Walt should be back in the neck with a posse. Even if they got out of the neck with their laden wagons, possemen on horseback should not have much trouble overtaking them. But a gunfight was exactly what he had wanted to avoid. Eventually, forted-up outlaws inside war wagons would have to yield. Even if they had stores of food and water in there with them. It might take longer if they were provisioned, but the end would be the same.

Walt spat and swore to himself. What he had planned had been a clean capture, no gunfire, full recovery of the stolen bullion, and a quiet parade down through Peralta from the north with prisoners being herded ahead, arms lashed behind their backs.

He was immersed in bitter reflections when Fred Tower roused him. "Walt! Look yonder—ahead a half-mile or so and out in front of us."

Kelly squawked before Walt could make them out: it looked like four men, one on a light saddle animal, another on a thirteen-hundred-pound team horse, and two other men with rifles in their hands standing beside the mounted men.

Walt yanked back to a dead halt. He knew they were safely beyond carbine range, but was less sure that they would be beyond rifle range.

Fred leaned on his mount's thick neck, squinted, then said, "They must've caught their harness-horse, or else they had another one we didn't see tied in the stand of trees back up behind the camp. They didn't waste any time catching a team horse and heading us off. Gents, I'll tell you what I think: those men don't have any intention of allowin' us to reach town . . . and they got a big advantage. We can't outrun 'em, can't outshoot 'em, and I never was worth a damn in a footrace."

The distant figures were unmistakably horses and armed men, but visibility was very poor at that distance. Walt looked left and right. That spit of trees was far back. There was a chance they might be able to reach it before they were run down and shot. Not a very good chance, but a chance, and in any other direction there was nothing to hide behind to enable three men riding worn-down big team horses to flee from the outlaws who had out-maneuvered them. They had been watching the backtrail. The outlaws had ridden hard to get ahead, and when they knew they were far enough in the lead, they had ridden down into plain sight, in front of the men they were hunting.

One of the men on the ground handed his rifle to the other dismounted man and said something to the rider of the saddle horse, who immediately dismounted. The unarmed man mounted the saddle horse and set his animal into a walk directly toward Fred, Kelly, and Walt.

None of them made a sound. When the horseman was close enough for the men from Peralta to be sure of his identity, he reined to a halt, raised his right hand, and called ahead. "It's time for a little talk, gents." He lowered his arm and sat like a statue, evidently awaiting a reply.

Walt muttered to his companions under his breath, "We're going to lose if we don't."

Fred nodded stiffly. "Let him come."

Walt raised his voice. "Come ahead, Warren."

The bulky, dark man said, "I'll meet you out here, Constable."

Walt kneed his big horse ahead at a slow walk. Neither he nor the large man took their eyes off each other until Walt halted about fifteen feet from the swarthy man and nodded. Ralph Warren put both hands on the large saddlehorn and smiled. "I got a lot of questions, Constable, but right now they aren't important. . . . You're not going any farther. If you try, you'll get yourself and your friends shot." Warren waited a moment, then resumed speaking. "We'll round up the horses you ran off but it'll take time, and we'll move out as soon after that as we can. You know I can't let you reach Peralta, but I don't want to kill you either, so if you gents will throw down your guns we'll take you back to the spring an' when we pull out we'll leave you up there tied and gagged. . . . Constable, I had some trouble convincing my men not to kill you."

Walt glanced past where the three outlaws were waiting, guns in hand. He swung his attention back to the outlaw chieftain. "You'll never make it," he said. "Sooner or later we'll reach Peralta."

Warren shrugged beefy shoulders. "Maybe. But you'll be alive. Now toss down that six-gun. I don't like to waste time, Constable."

Walt studied the big man. Warren's expression was relaxed and confident. Warren had something in mind. He had known since leaving Gloria with his load of bullion ingots that he could not possibly outrun anyone who came after him. It had been said of Ralph Warren, more properly Paul Lightle, notorious and successful outlaw, that he was very clever. Walt let his breath out slowly. With a slow reach he lifted out the six-gun and let it drop.

Warren's wide smile returned. He twisted in the saddle and raised an arm, signaling his companions to approach. He then straightened up in the saddle and told Walt to call his companions out to the rendezvous.

Walt obeyed and privately hoped very hard that irascible Fred Tower would not do anything rash. Warren spoke amiably to Walt.

"You're a smart man, Constable. I'd have had to kill the three of you. Your friends should be grateful."

Kelly and Fred came up riding double on the big sorrel horse, and Warren looked at them as though he would laugh. Instead he explained the conditions by which they would be kept alive, then pointed to Walt's gun in the grass and told them to throw down their carbines.

Kelly obeyed without a word. Fred did too, but for a moment Walt was not sure he was going to; he glared at Ralph Warren. The big man smiled back. "Good thing you got pig-headed over that land in town," he told Fred. "If you'd agreed to sell it to me I'd have had to hand over good money . . . I didn't want that damned land."

"Then why did you raise such a ruckus when I wouldn't sell it to you?" Fred asked.

Warren's riders came up, halted, and with their guns in hand, looked and listened. "Because," explained the outlaw, "McGregor had to believe everything I told him about starting up a stage company in his town. That was the only piece of ground anyone would want if they figured to make a corralyard on Main Street." Warren paused, enjoying his private joke, then went on speaking. "McGregor sent two testimonial letters to the executives of the big mine south of Gloria. One letter was about my plans for a local stage line. The other letter was about me havin' a big account in the Peralta bank and being known to him as the representative of some rich eastern investors."

Walt could not resist asking a question. "Why Peralta; why not make out like you were going to start up a stageline down at Gloria? It would have been a lot closer."

Warren eyed him disdainfully. "Gloria already has a stage company, but even if it didn't have, Constable, I've been in this business a long time; I can tell you being a stranger with a lot of financial backing works best from a distance." Warren raised his rein hand. "You gents ride out front. We're going back to that spit of trees, up through there to the ridge and along the ridge to the spring on the sidehill where the wagons are. We left a man back there to get things ready. We can move out one wagon. As soon as daylight comes we'll round up those horses you turned loose back yonder and move out the second wagon."

The man named Herman Smith dismounted and collected their carbines from the ground. When he was on his horse again, Warren motioned for Walt to lead the way.

Walt turned and started toward the trees. He was still having trouble believing Warren would be able to disappear with a pair of big, massive war wagons loaded with stolen bullion bars.

What worried him most was the fact that he really believed Warren could do it.

As they were turning up through the trees to rising ground, that muscular, slow-moving man rode up beside Walt and looked sardonically at him. "You never had a chance, Mister," Smith said. Walt gazed stonily at the man and said nothing.

The night was cold now; that paleness to the sky had increased. Dawn was close. Kelly O'Bryon's big horses plodded doggedly along; the men on their backs showed the same lack of spirit. Kelly was riding beside the *vaquero* when he said, "You got any jerky?" The Mexican dug out two twisted, lint-encrusted, nearly black sticks and silently handed them over. Kelly thanked him and offered the second stick to Fred, who was riding in front, and went to work on the other stick himself.

They were in sight of the sidehill camp when the man who had been left behind to harness the horses turned to watch them approach. He too was a Mexican.

When they all swung to the ground, Warren handed the reins of the saddle horse to the second Mexican and told him in Spanish to ride back, find the horses the men from Peralta had been driving, and bring them to camp.

Smith carried the carbines to the second war wagon and set them inside.

Warren took Walt up to the front wagon, motioned for him to climb, and when they were both standing on the high seat looking down into the wagonbed, Warren snagged a soiled old canvas with a long hook and yanked the canvas away.

Walt felt his breath stop for a moment. He had known the war wagons were heavily laden, and he had known they were carrying bullion bars, but he was not prepared for what he saw: two rows of silver bars aligned across the bottom of the wagon, and above them, smaller, another two rows of solid gold bars. Each had been stamped while soft with some initials, numbers, and what was probably the trademark of the mine where the metal had been melted and formed into ingots.

Warren laughed and tapped Walt's arm. "You know how much money that amounts to?"

Walt had no idea and shook his head as Warren used his hook to yank the old tarpaulin back over the bars. "Neither do I, Constable, but it's more'n most men would earn in maybe twenty lifetimes."

They climbed down. Warren dusted his hands, watched his men striking camp, and considered Fred and Kelly, who had not been invited to view the stolen fortune. He took all three of them to a large grub box and told them to open it and help themselves. He said they looked like they were starving. He was about half right; they weren't starving but they had not eaten in so long their stomachs probably thought their throats had been cut.

Fred said nothing, he simply ate. Kelly ate too, but showed lively interest in everything that was happening around them. He asked if Walt thought the outlaws would be able to find their missing horses.

Fred answered around a mouth full of food. "You're the horse expert, Kelly, what do you think?"

"I think they'll find them . . . Hand me that sourdough crust, Fred."

After locating the crust and passing it along, Fred chewed in thought, swallowed, and gazed at Constable Cutler. "Well, it's not as bad as last time you dragooned me'n Kelly into helpin' you, but that's not your fault, is it?"

Walt chewed, eyed his friends, and looked up as Ralph Warren came up with one of his men, the burly gunman named Smith, and several lengths of coiled rope. Warren made a motion and said, "Hands behind your backs. Tie 'em good, Herman." Warren walked away and the hulking outlaw worked without speaking, but when he had them all tied with their arms in back and their ankles lashed tightly, he leaned on one knee, looking at them with a faint smile. "Good try, boys; what you should have done was run them horses clean out of the country." He got to his feet with three soiled rags and gagged them, after which he threw them a mocking salute and walked away.

CHAPTER 19
Gone!

THE first war wagon rolled westward down past the site of last summer's cabin fire and on out of the neck using the same ruts it had used coming into the neck. The prisoners watched, as did the Mexican they had left behind with the second wagon.

There was nothing to say and if there had been they could not have said it anyway. The Mexican eyed them occasionally as he puttered around the camp waiting for the other *vaquero* to arrive with the loose stock.

The chill increased. Walt and Kelly had coats. Fred, who had used his coat to wrap the feet of the saddle horse, shivered and glared. He was the first of them to detect the approach of the Mexican driving the loose horses. Fred growled behind his gag and moved his head in the direction of the noise.

The rider was taking his time, perhaps because in semi-darkness he was afraid he might lose the team horses.

His countryman sang out in Spanish, and although the horseman was a considerable distance away, in the clear, utterly still predawn his words carried. The rider stood in his stirrups looking in the direction of the burned cabin. Then he sat down and called back.

When the loose horses came close the Mexicans caught them with as little effort as Walt, Fred, and Kelly had crept up on them last night. The Mexicans were in good spirits. As they heaved heavy harnesses on the large animals they gazed at the fuming, trussed captives and made jokes about them in Spanish. Fred was red in the face. He had been struggling with all his strength to get some slack in the ropes behind his back. He had perhaps an inch or two of slack. Beyond that the ropes refused to stretch. But what really annoyed him was that he understood their jokes.

Walt waited until the Mexicans were ready to back the wheelers onto the pole, then made loud noises behind his gag. The Mexicans regarded him impassively until his obvious urgency made them exchange a glance, and the man called Charlie walked over, stood briefly looking down, then with a shrug stepped back and untied the gag.

Walt spat twice and looked up at the *vaquero*. The question he asked made the Mexican scowl. "How far from here to the Mex border?"

The second Mexican walked over, but he could not speak English so his friend translated, and he answered curtly in Spanish. Charlie said, "Two days' ride. Why? You ain't going nowhere."

Walt spat again; the gag had been dirty. He looked at the pair of dark men. "Do you both have saddle horses?"

"No," replied Charlie. "We got one saddle horse."

"Any of those team horses broke to ride?"

Charlie answered slowly, looking more puzzled by the moment. "One of them is. The leggy, light horse." He interpreted for his friend, who made a remark that made Charlie laugh as he looked down at Constable Cutler. "Why? You want to buy him?"

"No, and you won't have to buy him either." He paused, looking from one Mexican to the other. "How long you been working for Warren?"

Charlie shrugged. "We didn't work for him. He hired us to drive his wagons from a town near the border up to Gloria. After that—he said if we'd go with him to Denver he'd pay each of us two hunnert dollars."

Walt considered the stocky man. "You'd never live to reach Denver. And he's not goin' to Denver. He is stealing that bullion."

Charlie shrugged again. "We know that. It don't make any difference to us. He said he'd pay us to—"

"He'll keep you until he doesn't need you any more, then they'll bury both of you under a mound of rocks."

The taller Mexican plucked at Charlie's sleeve for an interpretation, and after Charlie had given it, the tall man stared at Walt and said something only Charlie could hear. He translated it. "He says you're lyin' because you think you can talk us into untying you."

Walt looked squarely at the tall Mexican. "Naw. I'm not lying, and you don't have to turn us loose. We'll take care of that after you're gone—and with wagons like those that can't move any faster'n a walk, someone will overtake you—maybe you and Charlie will be shot in the back by then, but either way you're going to lose; either they'll kill you so you can't tell anyone what you've been doing, or a posse of riders will do it for Warren." Walt waited until all that had been translated, then did not allow the tall Mexican to try a rebuttal. He spoke to Charlie again.

"Two hundred dollars? Even if he gave it to you . . . Charlie, we'll do better. You and your friend saddle two horses, cut us loose, we'll break one of the bars in two, each of you take one half and ride south to the line. We won't tell anyone where you went. No one will even know you're gone for at least one full day . . . Charlie, one half of one of those gold bars is worth a hell of a lot more than two hundred dollars."

Again Charlie had to interpret. This time when he finished, the tall Mexican's gaze at Walt was far less antagonistic, but he gestured with both arms and spoke a volley of excited Spanish. Charlie groaned aloud and interpreted. "He says why should we settle for just one bar split between us when we could take it all, if that's what we decide to do?"

Walt shook his head. "One bar of gold is heavy as hell. If each of you carry half you won't overburden your horses. If you try to take more and get greedy, you'll never even make it as far as Gloria . . . Charlie, climb into that wagon and lift one of those gold bars."

Charlie did not move. He told his companion what Cutler had said, and the tall Mexican turned thoughtful. He seemed to already know the weight of a gold ingot. After a moment he flapped his arms and said something brusque.

Charlie hung fire before interpreting, acting as though what he had to say made him uncomfortable. ". . . All right. But just you climb in and throw out the bar. I'll keep a gun on your friends." Charlie spoke aside in Spanish. The tall man drew a wicked-bladed boot-knife and carelessly slashed their ropes. Kelly rubbed his freed arms and worked his fingers. Fred fished for his plug and worried off a corner without taking his eyes off the pair of Mexicans. Then he smiled and said in Spanish, "You are very wise horsemen. For each of you half of one of the gold bars will settle you in riches. You can become great land owners."

The tall Mexican's interest in Fred was obvious. He spoke to him. "What will you do after we depart—race for Peralta and get armed men to go with you after us?"

Fred laughed as he wagged his head. "Let me tell you, companion: It is not our gold either. My friend here is an honest man; you will ride with God and be tranquil. We will say absolutely nothing."

The tall man's black eyes sparked. "You will then take all the rest of the bars? Someday you will become *presidente* of all New *Mejico*. No?"

Fred lurched up to his feet laughing. Walt and Kelly also arose, but they said nothing, simply stood gazing in wonder at their old friend. To Walt's knowledge he had never heard the harnessmaker even swear in Spanish. From Kelly's expression the surprise was mutual.

Fred went over to slap the tall man on the shoulder. "When I am *presidente* I will hunt for you. You will become *comandante* of the entire south desert."

Both Mexicans laughed. Fred turned to Walt. "Get their gold bar," he said in English, and waited until Walt and the tall Mexican were walking toward the war wagon before addressing Charlie, this time in English. "He told you the truth. Warren would have shot both of you, sure as hell. Dead men couldn't tell where he took the stolen bullion, could they?"

Charlie seemed disinclined to shed his loyalty so quickly. He was watching Walt climb up the side of the big wagon as he replied to the harnessmaker.

"He didn't shoot you an' he had reason to. Buck and Herman wanted him to let them do it."

"Buck and Herman," stated Fred Tower sourly, "would shoot a man at the drop of a hat. There's another one like them. He's locked in the Peralta jailhouse. Warren would only have to nod his head, Charlie. He wouldn't do it himself, but it would be done."

Walt threw the gold bar to the ground and climbed down after it. The tall Mexican was lifting it, hefting its weight. As he did this he turned, smiling broadly in Charlie's direction. In Spanish he said, "Very heavy."

Charlie stared at the gold bar like a man in hypnosis. Not until Fred spoke to him in Spanish did he look away from the gold. "We need a way to cut the bar into halves, friend."

It was easier to do than any of them thought it might be. The tall Mexican made slow cuts crossways with his dagger, each time leaning more of his weight downward. Then he raised the bar in both hands, looked for a rock, and brought it down hard over stone. The bar broke cleanly in the middle.

Each Mexican lifted one half of the bar. They balanced the weight, probably making rough and no doubt crude estimates of its weight, struggling to translate that into pesos.

The tall man gazed at his half of the gold bar and muttered a small prayer of thanks, then arose and jerked his head at Charlie. "Let us went," he said in barely understandable English. Charlie took his half of the ingot with him as the two of them went after the horses.

Walt stared at Fred Tower. Fred saw his expression and looked uncomfortable. "Well, if you'd spent as much time around 'em as I have, you'd pick up the lingo. It's easy to learn." Then Fred changed the subject. "Now what? Head for town?"

Walt nodded. "After they leave. But just one of us, because sure as hell Warren's going to start sweating when this wagon doesn't come up where he can see it."

Fred nodded and looked around. "Guns," he murmured. Walt ignored that as he looked at O'Bryon. "You go to Peralta, Kelly. Tell McGregor at the bank what happened out here—get everyone you can and bring them back loaded for bear." Walt turned to watch the pair of Mexicans get astride. The light draft horse the tall Mexican was astride rolled its eyes until the Mexican got it untracked and although the three watching men would have wagered money the draft horse was going to buck, the Mexican was no novice. He knew how to prevent that, and he did it; he turned the horse left, then right to get it moving, and after it was lined out he did not allow it time to think of anything else. As he and Charlie rode past the men from Peralta they grinned, called out, laughed, and kept on going southward, up over the low hill that blocked the neck from that direction, and from the ridge they both turned to wave, then disappeared down the far side.

Kelly went after one of his sorrel horses. As he was leading it back he pointed. "The carbines," he said.

Fred retrieved the weapons, checked them both for loads, and was returning from the wagon as Kelly and Constable Cutler spoke briefly before Kelly also rode toward that low southward hill.

Walt took the gun the harnessmaker held out to him. He watched the world beyond the neck brighten with new-day sunlight, considered Fred Tower, and wagged his head. "You are loaded with surprises," he told the older man, as he led the way over to the wagon.

They searched for food, found some, sat in warming sunlight on the near side of the wagon, and watched the team horses, which were supposed to be pulling the war wagon, wander aimlessly in tall grass.

About a mile southward where black char from the burned cabin looked stark in sunlight, an old, shaggy dog-wolf was prowling. They watched him. Fred doubted that he would make it through another winter. Walt nodded in agreement. The wolf pawed in the burned debris, gave that up, and went over to scratch in layers of dust in the sagging woodshed. He got a mouse started. The men ate and watched as the wolf turned, sucked back, sprang ahead, and finally overtook the mouse midway betwen the shed and the cabin site. Walt said, "He needs a lot more than one mouse."

Fred wiped both hands on his shirt, tipped his hat lower to ward off sunlight, and blew out a big breath. "You got any idea how much bullion we are leaning against?"

". . . A thousand pounds?"

"More than that, Walt. A wagon like this could haul an even ton—with four big horses out front. How much would a ton of that stuff come to in dollars, do you expect?"

Fred turned his head to gaze at the older man. He had no idea how much money a ton of gold and silver would bring in greenbacks, nor did it interest him right at this time. "Don't get too comfortable," he said, "It'll take Kelly an hour to reach town, another hour maybe to get up a posse, and another hour to get back here . . . I just plain don't believe Warren is goin' to wait that long before he comes chargin' back lookin' for this wagon—and we got two carbines."

Fred continued to lean, eyes narrowed, face shaded from sunlight. "Two carbines—and this war wagon . . . I think you're right, that slippery devil will come back." Fred continued to gaze down where the rheumatic lobo was stirring clouds of dust in the woodshed looking for another mouse. "I got to say this for Warren: he's not a killer."

Walt did not believe men like Warren ever were killers. Not in the way men like Jack Pinter, Buck Jensen, and Herman Smith were killers. "He doesn't have to be, Fred. He hires men for that."

Fred groped for his plug, offered it, and when Walt made a negative sound Fred went to work worrying off a cud for himself. Afterwards, while pocketing the plug, he said, "That's another thing. Women don't like chewin' tobacco."

Walt scanned the distant open land beyond the neck as he replied. He did not particularly care for it either, and that included being with men who chewed, but in a country where every other man used plug tobacco, he kept his dislike to himself.

Fred turned discreetly aside, sprayed amber, and settled forward again. "I'll tell her I chew," he said.

Walt dryly replied to that. "You do that, only unless she is blind she already knows it."

Fred's eyes widened slightly. "You reckon?"

"How in the hell could she not know, Fred? She's been around you for years. Everyone knows you chew. Bertha knows too, sure as hell."

Fred dwelt on that for a while, then brightened. "Well now, if she knows, and she still sort of admires me, why then I don't see where there is goin' to be a fight, do you?"

Walt continued to watch the far country. "Unless she's got in mind making you over. I've been told they do that; marry a man, warts and all, because they figure to make him into something that—maybe—don't chew tobacco."

Fred's bright expression faded slowly, he spat again, then mumbled, "Walt, I wish you hadn't said that."

They had to move: the sun heat bounced off the massive oaken wagon-sides, making it hot where they had been sitting. They climbed to the high seat with their carbines, but delayed sitting up there until they had climbed down inside the wagonbed and pulled back the soiled canvas.

Fred swallowed hard, his Adam's apple bobbed, and his habitually squinted eyes sprang wide. For a moment he was speechless, then he said, "It's got to be at least a ton, Walt. I never in my life saw anything like it." He looked at one of the neat rows. There was a vacant place. He raised his head in Walt's direction. "What will you tell those mine-company officials about their missing bar of gold?"

"The truth; we split it between two Mexicans in exchange for them setting us loose."

"Walt, don't you expect they're goin' to say that was a hell of a lot of money to give away just so's we could get untied?"

"Fred, we were out here, they weren't. And I'd say that would be a cheap price to pay to get back the rest of it—but most of all I don't care a tinker's damn what they say . . . Fred?"

"What?"

"Do you hear horses?"

CHAPTER 20
Winners and Losers

THE sun was in their faces but that was not what made them halt three abreast out at the entrance into the neck. Sunlight or no sunlight, they could see their second wagon up there at the spring with its tongue on the ground and team harness in a tangled mound while the horses who were supposed to be wearing it were peacefully grazing north of the big pine trees.

Walt sighed as he watched them sitting out there in broad daylight. Warren was in the middle. Buck Jensen was on his right, Herman Smith was on his left. Fred studied them for a while, then said, "There's no one with the other wagon."

Walt did not see that as worth commenting about. Even if they hadn't hidden the other wagon, there was very little likelihood of anyone coming across it out here where the nearest buildings were miles westward.

"Sure, takin' their time," Fred muttered.

"They got reason to," Walt replied. "They can see the wagon up here, along with the harness horses—but no Mexicans and no prisoners tied up sittin' on the ground."

Fred pulled back from the rifle-barrel hole in the high, reinforced side of the war wagon. The sun was fierce down in there. He used an old faded bandana to mop off sweat as he said, "They only got two choices that I can see. Try to rout us out of here and drive away with their rig, or forget all about it an' go back an' be satisfied with just one wagonload of bullion."

Constable Cutler snorted. "Do you think Warren would give up that easy? I don't."

"How long has Kelly been gone?"

Walt made a guess. "Maybe an hour."

"Good. By now he'd ought to be in town raisin' hell and propping it up."

Walt also had to lean back from his gun hole and wipe sweat off his face. "I got a feeling, Fred, that by the time Kelly gets up here with a posse, whatever is going to happen will have happened."

Finally, after what seemed to be a discussion, the three horsemen in the distance split up. One rider went over in the direction of the low hill that ran along the full distance of the neck to the south. Another horseman turned in the opposite direction. The slightly higher hill he was aiming for protected the neck on its north side. Over there, the underbrush and timber were thicker than on the stump-ground of the southward hill.

One man remained out in the clear west of the cabin site. Neither of the men forted up in the war wagon had any difficulty identifying him, even at that distance. Ralph Warren—or Paul Lightle—was larger and thicker than either of his companions. Fred squinted through his loophole. "You know," he said quietly, "if I had one of them rifles those fellers carry, I believe I could hit him from here."

There was a canteen in the front boot below the high seat. Walt crawled up, got it, and came back down. He and Fred drank with the usual result; more perspiration than before poured out of their hides.

By noon with the sun directly overhead it was going to be like an oven inside the wagon. Fred shook off sweat and leaned to peer through his gun hole again. There was no sight of Warren. The harnessmaker reared back and scanned the high sides. "One of us better keep watch up there, or sure as hell they'll sneak up and shoot us down in here like frogs in a a sump hole." Fred stood in thought, then spoke again. "Who in hell figured men would be safe in one of these wagons? If a sniper don't shoot you from above, the sun'll fry your brains."

Walt turned with a grin. "Maybe that wouldn't take long."

Fred scowled and leaned to peer out his gun hole again. The land was empty, even the old lobo wolf had departed. He stepped back and sat down atop the soiled old canvas, fidgeted, and glanced at Constable Cutler. "Did you ever expect to sit on more gold an' silver than most folks ever see an' not be able to benefit from it? Besides that, it's harder than a rock." Fred arose and stepped over to his hole again, but the neck of land, broad and deep and heavily grassed, remained utterly empty.

Walt moved over to a gun hole beneath the high seat. It was higher than the sideboard holes because of the footrest above the leather boot. He carried four silver bars over, stacked them and climbed up. With an unimpaired view northward now, he was able to scan about half of that east-west rib of hillside that protected the neck on the north.

Fred did the same at the high tailgate, but back there he did not have to stand on anything. As much of the cut-over, lower hill southward as he could see showed nothing. No rider and no movement. He spat, turned, and said, "They're not goin' to ride up here, they're goin' to skulk."

He was correct: a large rock sailed up over the high oaken sideboard from the east and landed among the ingots with a loud noise. One of the outlaws had gotten completely around the wagon up the brushy sidehill in that direction and had lobbed a rock, probably for reaction. It did not seem to Walt that the outlaws would believe the war wagon was empty, but if neither he nor Fred made any noise after the rock landed, possibly the rock-thrower would begin to wonder if there was anyone inside.

A half-hour passed with neither of the men inside the wagon seeing movement until someone pelted the grazing horses with stones, and this time, the harness animals ran, Kelly's remaining big sorrel horse among them. Walt watched the horses rush down as far as the old cabin site before stopping and thought whoever had done that had been foolish; neither he nor Fred could have used those horses so there was no point in running them off. Also, the rock-thrower let the forted-up men know he was out there.

The stillness continued, the sun climbed, those distant horses were ambling toward the open range beyond the neck, and two circling buzzards made several sweeps above the meadow before allowing themselves to be borne farther away by high winds.

Walt stepped away from his hole, squinted at the sun, which was almost directly overhead, and saw Fred step back to face him. Fred pantomimed a man lifting out his pocket watch, opening it, reading the hands, then replacing the watch in his pocket. Walt held up two fingers. It was his guess that about two hours had passed since Kelly had ridden away. Fred nodded and faced the tailgate again.

Clearly, the harnessmaker was putting his faith in the arrival of a posse from Peralta. Walt would have said nothing derogatory about that, but he did not believe the outlaws were going to let much more time pass.

The rock-thrower was northward when he sailed several more large stones down inside the war wagon. Walt shook his head; the man was not going to hit anyone with his rocks, although he might make the forted-up men apprehensive. Maybe that was his intention. Walt thought the man was trying to provoke some kind of response to satisfy himself there actually were men in the wagon.

Unexpectedly, a deep voice sang out from along the north slope, where underbrush and timber were thick enough to hide the caller.

"You in the wagon! Listen to me! This is Lightle talking. Ralph Warren to you. I got two sticks of dynamite. Maybe I won't get the first one inside but if it lands within fifty yards of the wagon it'll seem like the end of the world—an' I still got another stick. You hear me?"

Walt looked back. Fred was watching him. He raised a finger to his lips, and the harnessmaker nodded, just once.

The outlaw called again. "I'm not goin' to give you another chance. Throw out your guns and climb out. Otherwise, I'll pitch the first stick of dynamite over."

Walt turned as Fred Tower came up beside him. Fred looked skeptical. "He don't have any dynamite. Where would he get it?"

Walt agreed, but privately he had learned not to undersell Ralph Warren. In this case, he just might actually have dynamite.

The deep voice sang out for the last time. "Don't think I'm bluffing. Climb out of there."

Fred was beginning to look definitely worried. Walt brushed his arm and shook his head. "Even if he has it, Fred, if he tossed a stick in here he'd blow chunks of gold and silver all over the countryside. He knows that. Go watch through the tailgate. There's one over there somewhere."

After Fred departed, Constable Cutler eased his carbine barrel through the hole a few inches, testing to see if he could turn it as far westward as the sound of that voice had been. He couldn't. Leaning the gun aside he stepped onto the bullion bars, peered out, and saw something thick and bulky making underbrush quiver along the slope. He watched it, knowing very well that whatever it was, it was beyond accurate carbine range.

Ralph Warren did not call out again. The sun finally reached its zenith, sweat was running in rivulets off the men down in the war wagon, and Walt turned to look upwards along the high sides of the wagon, which were a foot and a half higher than his head.

Something was moving along the near side of the rig. He could occasionally detect abrasive sounds. Fred was fully occupied back beside the tall tailgate and did not even look around as Walt began very carefully inching along the side-board on his left.

Whoever had managed to crawl up this close had done so when Warren had distracted the hidden men inside the wagon. Walt shook off sweat and wagged his head. Every time he and Warren met, it seemed that the outlaw outsmarted the constable.

Dump-wagons had two reinforced panels running the full length of their beds. Ordinarily there was a round steel rod running from the back to the front that served as the trip of the panels. If the rod could be released, both the panels would drop open. Most of the steel rods were notched so that the amount of discharge from the belly of the wagon could be regulated from either a very thin spill of rocks or sand or gravel, to a deluge if the rod was pulled completely free, allowing both panels to spring wide open.

Walt had no idea what the man against the near-side wall of the wagon was up to, but with a strong suspicion he leaned to move eight heavy bars of bullion until he could see the dump-rod through a slit in the floorboards.

When he looked up, Fred was raising his carbine very gently, while keeping one eye to the gun hole in the tailgate. If Fred had detected one of the stalkers, Walt was confident he knew where another one was. He knelt very carefully, waited until he could hear someone softly grunting as he bellied his way beneath the wagon. Then Walt used his Winchester barrel to reach down, rest it against the round steel rod, and wait.

He was leaning down when a gun barrel was worked up from beneath. It was a very tight fit. Walt leaned closer. For seconds his left eye and the right eye of the straining man eighteen inches below met in a blinkless stare, then Walt heaved all his weight on the carbine, the steel rod buckled, tore loose, and as both floorboard panels crashed open a man screamed.

A ton of bullion bars went down through the floorboards with a muffled roar like thunder, and the big wagon shuddred violently, dust arose from below, and Fred almost lost his footing as he whirled around.

Walt leaned back, blinking in the dust. Over the crashing

echo a man's startled outcry sounded from over among the trees and underbrush on the north sidehill.

Fred Tower ignored clouds of dust rising inside the war wagon to stare up where Walt was sitting back on his heels. Dust arose above the high sideboards, was still rising as the last of the echoes died.

Walt got to his feet holding the carbine and looking down. All that was visible was an immense tumble of dully gleaming bullion bars, and a man's upturned hand forming a wildly curled claw.

Fred said, "What happened?"

Walt did not reply, he turned back toward the gun hole beneath the wagon seat and looked out. There was a flatly spreading thin drift of dust in the still, hot autumn afternoon, otherwise there was nothing to be seen, no shadow and no movement.

Fred remained transfixed for a moment longer, then faced the tailgate again, but this time he did not raise his Winchester. If the stealthy movement he had seen out there had been a man, he was gone.

The dust was a long time settling. There was a deeper silence now than there had been. Down by the cabin site the underground reverberations of all that weight falling freely to the ground had panicked the team horses. They had their heads and tails up as they raced toward the open range beyond the neck.

The wagon was riding higher on its springs now. It was also listing slightly downhill, impelled in that direction by the weight which had raised it from below a little, in that direction.

Walt wilted a little from the heat and other things. After another half-hour had passed, he turned and spoke quietly to Fred, explaining what he had done and why he had done it. He also moved along the outward-leaning west side of the wagon and peered through a gun port in the direction of the cabin site and the swaybacked woodshed.

One man was walking out of the northward underbrush down there, trailing a long-barreled rifle in his meaty fist. He was large and thick. He did not look up toward the wagon. He did not look in the direction of the southerly hill, either. He went directly to the back of the woodshed and vanished from Walt's sight, but not for very long. When he emerged he was astride a big harness horse riding west toward open country.

Fred came over to an adjacent gun hole and also watched Warren leaving the neck. He said, "He's quitting, Walt. By Gawd, it's hard to believe. He's riding away." Fred stopped speaking briefly, then leaned far to his right in order to take in more of the cut-over southward low hill. "Watch," he said. "Watch over near where them big bushes grow over some tall stumps."

Evidently the man who had been stalking the wagon from that other hill was also leaving, probably because he had seen Warren's departure. But this man was much more careful. He did not expose himself to the watchers in the wagon until he was down near the burned cabin, and even then when he strode in the direction of the woodshed and disappeared around behind it where evidently his horse had also been tethered, he moved swiftly and in a zigzag fashion, even though he really had very little to fear from the watchers in the wagon, who only had carbines.

Walt said, "You recognize him, Fred?"

The harnessmaker nodded. "Herman Smith."

They watched the gunman emerge from behind the woodshed astride another big harness horse. He rode westward in the wake of Warren without once looking back over his shoulder.

Fred shook off sweat. "For just two minutes I'd like to have one of their rifles."

CHAPTER 21
Tired Men

HEAT was a problem. Even though Walt and the harnessmaker did not believe Warren or his gunfighter would return, they were not ready to leave the wagon. Walt stood on the bullion bars to examine the countryside while Fred went over where the big ingots had fallen through the floorboards, saw the claw-shaped hand and knelt to see if he could locate the rest of the dead man. He could have if he'd wanted to move nearly a ton of dead weight in the kind of heat inside the wagon that made moving at all seem like real labor. He stood up, absent-mindedly dusted his knees, and moved away. The crushed gunman was Jensen, the younger of Warren's gunguards, or whatever they actually were.

Walt drank and passed along the canteen. As Fred tanked up and leaned the canteen in shade, Walt said, "I didn't expect him to pull out, but I'm not surprised that he did. He lost one man, which most likely didn't bother him a lot, but for him and Herman Smith to get us out of here—even if they could—would have shot most of the afternoon . . . Then they would have had to climb down in here and lift every one of those big bars and restack them. That'd take maybe until dusk. Then they'd have to find their harness-horses, fetch them back up here, rig them out, and get under way . . . The whole day would be wasted, Fred, and Warren would have realized that."

Fred thought Walt was about right. "The way he rode out of here—like a sleepwalker—did you see that? Like maybe he was stunned or maybe plumb demoralized."

They climbed gingerly toward the high seat, got down on the east, or uphill, side of the wagon, and dove into some underbrush where they remained for a long while. The world around them was silent. There was no movement. The air was clear but it still retained a faint scent of dust.

Fred got comfortable by stamping out a place with heavy boots. Walt looked at their carbines. Yesterday somebody had worried about not having any more bullets than were in the magazine of each Winchester—and they had not fired a shot.

He felt his face. It itched from beard stubble and sunburn. As the tenseness trickled away weariness replaced it. He was not hungry. He was not even very thirsty. But he felt tired all the way through.

Fred was leaning back, carbine across his lap, hands at rest atop it eyeing Walt. "What was that darned fool tryin' to do under the wagon?"

"Poke a gun barrel up through the floorboards."

Fred's expression turned saturnine. "What good would that do? He couldn't see to shoot anyone, even if he could jockey the damned gun far enough to the left or right . . . That was a hell of a way to die, regardless."

Walt did not dispute that. "There aren't too many good ways to die that I know of, Fred."

Tower thought about that, then straightened up slightly, and cocked his head. But it was a false alarm. It was horses all right, but they were not coming up-country across the stumpy lower hill. It was Warren's stampeded harness animals coming back up the neck from out on the open range. They had Kelly's big sorrel horse with them.

Fred settled down with an impatient curse. "What's takin' Kelly so long?"

Walt shrugged and moved just enough to be out of direct sunlight, then relaxed again. "Something has been bothering me ever since we headed out here and saw Warren's wagons."

Fred's saturnine expression returned. "Yeah, somethin' bothered me too; gettin' out of this mess alive."

Walt seemed not to have heard. He fixed his gaze upon the older man as he spoke. "Where was he going?"

The harnessmaker considered the question while delving for what remained of his chewing plug. After emplacing the cud and pocketing what remained of his plug, he said, "You got an idea?"

Walt shook his head.

"Well then, I expect what we got to do when we get the chance is track down his damned wagon."

Walt accepted that suggestion because it had occurred to him earlier that it was about all he could really rely on. A large wagon as heavily laden as that one was would grind tracks into the ground a child could follow. But Warren would know that, and that was what had him puzzled. Warren was an experienced outlaw, smart as a wolf. If he left tracks he knew could be followed, he would have had something in mind to offset those tracks.

The second time Fred thought he heard horses it was indeed Kelly O'Bryon astride one of his livery animals leading a posse of what appeared to be no less than seven armed men. Walt got to his feet to watch Kelly break out over the ridge of the southerly hill, followed by other horsemen. Because they were bunched up it was difficult to make out their actual number, but once they were strung out Indian file behind O'Bryon, Walt could count them.

"Seven," he said and Fred Tower nodded his head, spat, and reached for the carbine before starting away from the brush clump behind Constable Cutler.

Kelly hesitated when he saw two men come from behind the wagon, then started forward again. Walt made out Pat Flannery from the saloon in town, the blacksmith and his helper, Jim McGregor riding with button shoes and a little dark derby hat and wearing a gunbelt around his middle. Beside the banker was a large stranger with a droopy moustache and a tipped-down dark hat, astride a powerful-looking gray horse.

The pair of riders bringing up the rear were local cowboys who had been in town when Kelly had arrived flushed, rumpled, and agitated. They had come along for the hell of it.

When everyone was on the ground, the pair of range-riders went over to stare at the leaning big war wagon. One of them hunkered down, made a whistling sound, and told his companion to look under there.

The blacksmiths and Pat Flannery also went over to stare at the war wagon, but Jim McGregor brought the darkly tanned stranger over to introduce him. He was an official from the mine south of Gloria. He did not say a word or smile as he pumped Constable Cutler's hand, then did the same with Fred Tower. Kelly had told them everything he knew back in town and had been answering questions all the way back to the neck. The tanned man asked about Warren. Walt told him what had happened, and that Warren and his remaining gunman had departed a couple of hours earlier. The mine official studied the westward flow of land between its two low hills, where he could see wagon tracks.

He went over to join the others looking at the wagon and beneath it. Jim McGregor remained with Walt and Fred. He shifted his gunbelt several times, unable to get comfortable with the thing. He probably had not worn a shellbelt and sidearm in many years. He raised the ludicrous little city hat, mopped sweat, lowered the hat, and said, "When Kelly come busting into the bank as Mr. Trent from the mine company and I was talking, I just couldn't believe it, Walt. I'd have staked my reputation on Mr. Warren."

Walt said, "You did, Jim. The next time someone rides into town lookin' big and successful, if I was in your boots I'd stay as far away from him as I could."

McGregor's normally pale face was flushed. He turned to look at the small crowd over beside the wagon. "Is all the bullion safe?" he asked.

"Maybe half of it, Jim. The rest of it is in another wagon. There is a dead man under those bullion bars. He got crushed when the bars dropped through the floorboards."

Fred Tower went over where Kelly and the saloonman were talking. Walt watched him go as he said, "Jim, there is something you might want to tell that man from the mining company. Maybe Kelly already told you."

"About the gold bar and the pair of Mexicans?"

"Yeah. Mr. Trent's company is going to be shy that much gold out of this wagon. I don't know anything about what's in the other wagon."

McGregor faced Constable Cutler. "He wasn't happy, Walt, Kelly said you did exactly right, otherwise Mr. Trent might not have got this much back. I guess that settled it."

Walt watched Trent and the pair of rangemen assessing the damage. Trent knew what had to be done. All of them knew that. The bars had to be taken from beneath the wagon, the floorboards had to be closed, horses had to be put onto the pole to pull the empty wagon clear, then the bars had to be handed up and over and down inside again. After that, Trent could head back to Peralta.

Pat Flannery walked over wagging his head. Before he could say anything, Walt stared at him as he said, "Who is lookin' after the jailhouse, my prisoner, and Frank Bellingham?"

Flannery gave a prompt reply. "Missus Bartlett and Bertha Maloney. I wanted to ride with the posse so they said they'd mind things."

Kelly left the men over at the wagon and pointed to the fresh horse he had ridden from town. "He'll pack double, Walt. You can ride back with me—unless you'd rather ride on the wagon with that feller from Gloria."

Walt's retort made the liveryman blink. "You ride back on the wagon, Kelly. I need that horse. Fred will be needing one too."

"For what?"

"To go find the other wagon and Warren."

Kelly stood gazing in silence at the dirty, unshaven, sunken-eyed man in front of him. "Let Flannery and the others do that," he said. "You need a decent meal and ten hours of sleep. You look like you been drug through a knothole."

Walt slapped the liveryman lightly on the shoulder as he walked past.

The mine company's official was already organizing a procedure for getting the bars from beneath the wagon, but only the pair of rangemen could actually climb under and push them out, and even they were mindful of the squashed man they were uncovering.

Fred was chewing and watching when Constable Cutler walked up. The harnessmaker turned and offered him two sticks of jerky the blacksmith's helper had given him. As Walt pocketed them he said, "See if Pat will loan you his gun and shellbelt. I'm going to borrow the one McGregor has. And borrow someone's saddle horse too."

Fred stopped chewing. His squinty eyes were fixed and motionless. "Why?" he asked quietly.

"Because we're going to find that other wagon."

Fred continued to regard Walt for a moment, then resumed masticating. "You never get enough, do you? Look around; everyone you see is in better shape than we're in."

Walt looked around. "Fred, they don't give a damn about Warren. If they did, they'd be riding out of here right now." He brought his gaze back to the harnessmaker.

Fred chewed and turned slowly back to watch the bullion bars being manhandled from beneath the wagon. He spat, then said, "If we ever get back to Peralta I'm goin' to tell Bertha I'll sell my harness shop if she'll sell her rooming house, and we can move so far away I'll never be friends with another constable as long as I live. . . . Where is Flannery? If I take his gun an' his horse, how is he goin' to get back?"

"On the wagon," stated Walt, and went over where the banker was sweating like a stud horse as he helped move the bullion bars.

McGregor was glad for the respite. As he straightened up

to listen to Walt Cutler, he mopped sweat off his red face and neck with a limp white handkerchief. Without a word he unbuckled the shellbelt, which was a damned nuisance anyway, and handed it over. Walt had to adjust the belt to its last hole and even then it was loose.

He went over where O'Bryon had tied his bay horse. As he was leading it over where Fred Tower was arguing with the saloonman, one of the rangemen beneath the wagon swore loudly and with feeling. He had uncovered the dead gunfighter, the man known as Buck Jensen.

Flannery was distracted by the cursing and turned away as Walt came up. Fred winked at him, tapped the saloonman's chest with a stiff finger to get his attention back, and said, "All right, Pat; you ride with the constable then, but I better tell you that son of a bitch with Warren is a gunfighter if I ever saw one."

Flannery looked at Walt, saw nothing in the lawman's face that even hinted of sympathy, growled curses, and removed his gunbelt. He pointed over where his horse was tied as he said, "You're a pair of idiots. If you'll wait a while, just until we get that bullion back into the wagon, and the horses on the pole so's Trent can head for town, the rest of us will go with you."

Walt slapped Flannery on the back as he had done the banker, and led the way over into tree shade where the saloonman's horse was dozing. He mounted Kelly O'Bryon's animal, found that the stirrups were too short, and let his feet dangle below them while he waited for Fred to recinch the other horse and lead it away from the tree before turning it twice, then swinging astride on the second turn.

Walt shook his head. "You didn't have to turn him. Kelly wouldn't ride a horse that bucked."

Fred looked from beneath this shapeless hat brim at the lawman. "Let me tell you something I learnt when you was wearing three-cornered pants. *Any* horse will buck."

They were midway between the war wagon and the

burned-out cabin when the mining-company official looked up from piling bullion bars, watched them for a moment, then said, "Where are they going?"

Pat Flannery answered him. "After the other wagon."

"Just the two of them?"

The blacksmith was shaking sweat off when he said, "That was all it took to get this one back, wasn't it? Besides, you're a stranger in these parts. Mister, if I was in trouble, them two'd be the gents I'd hunt up to help me out of it. . . . You want to finish here or stand there talking?"

Jim McGregor, who had been glad for this respite too, looked westward, where sunlight outlined the pair of riders, wagged his head, and bent down with a groan to resume piling bullion bars.

Walt and Fred rode in silence over the top of tire ruts leading past the cabin site toward the open range beyond that pair of hills which partially enclosed the Bartlett homestead. As they rode beyond the charred wreckage, Fred gazed at it, spat, and said, "I never had any desire to ride up in here again, after last year, an' I sure never expected to."

Constable Cutler did not turn his head in the direction of the burned-over place. "Something I figured out a few years back, Fred, is that about two-thirds of the time when a man gets up in the morning he wouldn't believe some of the things he'd do before nightfall."

CHAPTER 22
The Completed Circle

THE tracks were very plain underfoot and were also visible for several hundred yards ahead. They did not deviate. In the distance there was a range of mountains, and as far as Walt Cutler knew, there was no road over or through them this far west of the Peralta stage road. He jutted his jaw. "How does he think he's going through the mountains with that wagon?"

Fred's answer was accompanied by an upraised arm. "Somewhere up ahead, he's got to turn east. If there's a way through from the west I've never heard of it . . . Walt, he might have in mind abandoning the wagon and packing the bars on his team horses."

Cutler could not believe that. "He's only got four harness-horses. Even if he put two hundred and fifty pounds on each one—if his wagon is as loaded as that one was back in the neck—he'd have to leave about half his loot behind." As Walt finished speaking, he stood in his stirrups, but the tire tracks continued straight northward. He sat down and blew out a big sigh of exasperation.

They lifted the horses over into an easy lope, and that produced results: a mile and a half ahead with the nearing foothills showing brightly, the wagon tracks abruptly turned eastward. Fred crowed. "I told you. He's aimin' for the stage road north of town."

But he wasn't doing any such a thing. They adapted to the different direction and let the horses out a notch on this new trail in order to make time. They encountered pocked boulders of a brownish-grayish-bluish color. The farther they went, the more such rocks they encountered. Some were fist size; in other places they were as large as a man's head—at one point there was a pile of rock stacked up as big as a house.

Walt knew this area. Those scattered rocks could be found almost as far south as Peralta, but the closer one got to the foothills or the mountains, the thicker, and larger, they became. On his left, miles northward, was a series of up-thrust rims. At some time in a past too distant to be recalled, at least one of those peaks had erupted, shooting pumicelike pockmarked rocks for miles, like projectiles. The volcano seemed to be extinct, but the evidence that it had once been alive was scattered in all directions, and what Warren's laden wagon was doing now was zigzagging to avoid the largest rocks and straddling the smaller ones.

Fred was amazed. "The damned fool, he didn't have to come way up here before turning east to the road. By now he's got to be down to a crawl." As though to emphasize what Fred felt would reveal a distant wagon in view, he stood in his stirrups, but saw no wagon and sat down looking disappointed.

The sun was on their backs but it lacked the degree of heat they had suffered from earlier. What it did accomplish was equally as inconvenient: it made long shadows everywhere it struck one of the large volcanic boulders. It filled every swale with shadows, and it was beginning to shorten distant visibility.

An airborne sound came and went, bringing Walt fully alert. He knew the sound of chain harness and wagons crossing hard or stony ground. But it was a very distant sound, faint and illusive. He jerked his head and led off in a loose lope. There was no particular danger riding at a gallop through the rock field, but it was a good idea to watch carefully ahead, which both riders did, having had experience in this kind of terrain before.

Fred saw the wagon first and stood straight up in his stirrups to point it out to Constable Cutler. They settled into a steady gait. When the wagon was visible in detail no more than a mile ahead, Walt swore. "Only two horses on the tongue, Fred."

The harnessmaker said nothing, but kept his head tilted. Not only were two of the team horses missing, but as far as Fred could see, there was no one on the high driver's seat. He gestured for Walt to slack off. "If they're down inside they'll pick us off like grouse on a tree limb."

Walt dropped to a fast walk but he would have preferred to take a chance on being shot at by a gunman down inside the war wagon; exasperation made him impatient.

He watched the wagon. The horses pulling it were making decisions about which rocks to straddle and which ones to veer away from. He began to have a bad feeling. What made it stronger was when the team misjudged, allowed the near-side front wheel to strike a big rock and bounce back. The horses dropped into their collar pads and put their com-bined weight into forcing the wheel up atop the rock and down the other side with a loud noise. Walt did not know a teamster, and never had known one, who would encourage his horses to do something like that. Out here where there were no people for many miles, a broken wheel or a set of sprung wheel spokes meant one hell of a long walk for someone. He said, "Fred . . . there is no one in that wagon."

The harnessmaker leaned with both hands on the swells of his saddle and studied the distant rig with considerable interest. If there was no one down in the bed of the wagon, then where in hell were they? They certainly were not sitting on the high seat.

"Well, Constable," the older man said laconically. "This notion we had of trackin' down the wagon don't look as good to me now as it did a while back. You know why?"

Walt nodded. "They took two horses off the pole and got away."

Fred eased back down, robbed of his declaration. Consta-ble Cutler then made another observation and the harnessmaker forgot all about Warren and his gunman escaping. Walt said, "No two horses I ever saw could have dragged that wagon over a big rock—if there was anything in it."

They eased over into a lope, swerved away from one another when they were close enough to approach the team on either side. Blinders on the team's bridles prevented them from seeing in any direction but straight ahead, and until they heard riders sweeping up from the rear, the team plodded along. After they heard the riders, though, they came up into their collar pads ready to run.

It was too late. Walt swerved as close as he dared to the driver's side of the wagon, leaned to grip the steelwork of the binder-handle, and allowed the borrowed horse to run out from under him. He climbed up to the seat, freed the lines, and as the team started to break loose, he called down to them while easing back gently to bring them under control. They continued another ten or twelve yards, then responded to the tightened lines, and halted.

Walt looped the lines, and turned to look down into the wagonbed. It was empty except for a grub-box, which had been turned over when the rig had gone over that big rock, and a crumpled pile of stained wagon-canvas.

Fred climbed up on the far side, reached the boot, and leaned to also look downward. For a long time neither of them spoke. Fred turned, sat on the wooden seat, scanned the country in all directions, and spat in monumental disgust.

Walt's reaction was less disgust than bewilderment. He turned fully to look back. There was nothing back there but wagon tracks, shod-horse imprints, and rocks, large ones, small ones, and jumbles of them.

He looked downward again. "How the hell did they do it?"

Fred had both booted feet on the low dashboard, arms folded, leathery, weathered, sun-darkened face set in an expression of fierce resentment. "I'll tell you what they *didn't* do," he grumbled. "If there was as many of those damned bars in this wagon as there was in the other one, they sure as hell never got it all on two horses and made off with it." Having said that, Fred grudgingly stood up, turned, and looked down into the empty wagonbed again. As he was doing this he also grumbled. "How much lead they got on us? Maybe two hours since they quit back yonder and rode up to their damned wagon? Well, in two hours on big, clumsy pudding-footed draft horses a man would be pushed like hell to make ten miles. With a load, half that."

Walt arose to scan the empty land. He dropped his gaze to the pair of motionless team horses, then he started to climb down. Fred followed his example but without saying a word until they were back with their saddle animals, then he cocked an eye at his companion. "What do you think?"

"I think we got better horses, and I think if we find their tracks this time and daylight holds, we ought to be able to catch sight of them."

Fred nodded, but as he was riding past the wagon he halted, climbed down, unhitched the team from the wagon-tongue, carelessly swept the harness off over their rumps, removed the bridles, and slapped each horse lightly on the rump. He then got back astride and without speaking joined his companion.

They had to split up and quarter for almost a half-mile before Walt found the tracks he was seeking. He waved, and Fred loped over to join him.

This time they pushed the horses a little, each rider to one side of the shod-horse marks left by horses whose hooves were nearly twice the size of a saddle horse's hooves. The escaping men were going south. Fred scratched his head over that until Walt reminded him that so far, there had been a good reason behind whatever Warren had done.

The sun was lowering, those shadows among the volcanic boulders seemed to puddle in several directions now, and although visibility was decreasing, it was not doing it very fast. An hour along, the harnessmaker straightened up, satisfied that the draft-horse marks would not change course, looked all around, watched Walt for a moment, and said, "This is crazy, Walt. He's headin' straight for town."

Walt looked up from watching the tracks as they loped past them. "Not if you were straddling a fifteen-hundred-pound horse with someone chasing you. And it'll be close to dark by the time they get down there, Fred."

"What the hell for; they dassn't try to hide in—"

"To get fresh horses—faster and smaller ones. If they can manage that, we just darned well might not catch them— ever. Not if they can ride hard all night."

Fred loped for a few yards, then began shaking his head. "If I get anywhere near my shop with the bed in the back room, I'm going to be powerfully tempted to give up this life as a honorary constable, or whatever I been lately, and sleep for a week."

Walt was watching the tracks again. They were indeed aiming for Peralta and not over to the stage road to get down there. They were making a beeline run for it. He seemed engrossed with the tracks but he wasn't. He said, "Naw, you won't quit on me, Fred."

"No? Give me one reason why."

"Because I'll warn Bertha not to get into double harness with a man who gives up right when things are getting interesting."

"She knows me better'n that. She's known me for about fifteen years. Besides, you're gettin' the cart in front of the horse. Did I say I want to get into double harness with her?"

"Sure you did. Have you forgot that already?"

Fred paused a moment to reassure himself the tracks were still in front of them, then resumed the conversation. "I never in my life said any such a darned thing."

"The same as, Fred. We been on a manhunt since yesterday, been dodging and ducking killers, and every chance you've had since we came out here you've talked about Bertha Maloney."

The harnessmaker dropped his head and glared at the tracks in stony silence. His face was red beneath its perpetual tan but since Walt Cutler did not look up, he did not notice this.

They had been angling eastward as they had been loping southward, now a couple of miles north of town. They were closer to the stage road than they realized, until a noisy, old, faded coach went by and the driver raised his arm stiffly overhead in a salute. The distance was too great; he did not know who he was waving to, but it was a habit with him, as it was with most other stage drivers, to wave at horsemen along the way.

They waved back, and a mile farther along Walt slackened to a trot as he watched dust rising behind the stagecoach where it slackened speed on the edge of town.

Dusk was coming. In another hour or less it would arrive. Walt was looking down through town and allowed Fred to get him over parallel to the stage road before he said, "Fred, you stay up at this end of town. I'm going around to the west and get down behind the livery barn. Unless Kelly hired another hostler since we left yesterday, his barn is going to be wide open to anyone needing fresh horses. If they're down there I'll try to stop them. If they bust loose up this way, you do the same."

Fred watched Walt wheel around to his right and lift the horse he was riding into another loose lope. Fred went to the upper end of town north of the rooming house, where the plankwalks ended on both sides of Main Street, dismounted stiffly, genuflected his legs a couple of times, and looked for something to lean on. Down in front of Flannery's saloon a man Pat hired to stand in for him now and then came out front wearing his long white apron, adjusted two purple sleeve garters with embroidered white ruffles around their edges, glanced up and down the roadway as though impatient for customers to come along, then went back inside.

Fred could almost smell the musty, yeasty atmosphere of

the saloon and although he was not really a drinking man, if he hadn't felt a responsibility to stay where he was, he might have gone down there, bought a full quart, and taken it to the lean-to with him before retiring. It had been said that good malt whiskey never hurt anybody, and it had probably proven to be a better medicine than nine-tenths of the evil-smelling and worse-tasting elixirs medical doctors sold folks in little blue bottles for exorbitant prices.

Fred dug around for all that remained of his plug; just enough for one final chew. He tongued it into his cheek and held the reins to Pat Flannery's horse as he sank down upon the edge of the plankwalk.

CHAPTER 23
Peralta Again

IT was supper time in Peralta, the sidewalks were deserted, and most of the stores had been locked up for the night. The exceptions were the pool hall, the saloon, Kelly O'Bryon's barn at the lower end of town, and Elizabeth Bartlett's cafe.

Constable Cutler left his borrowed horse in a shed opposite the jailhouse across the alley and approached the livery barn through alley shadows. He was hoping with all his heart he would not be too late. Warren and Herman Smith could not have been too far ahead by the time Fred and Walt had reached town, but whether they knew they were being pursued or not, they would have a very good reason to want to saddle fresh horses and be on their way. He speculated that remounting might be delayed while they rigged out additional animals with pack saddles to carry their loot, although he was satisfied that they would not be carrying very much, if they were carrying any at all.

A large tan dog with a curving, upswept tail walked stiff-leggedly around someone's cow shed, stopped, and stared without making a sound or taking his tawny eyes off Constable Cutler.

Walt eyed him as he slipped past on the opposite, shadowy side of the alley. After he had passed, the tan dog turned and with considerable dignity and no haste went back toward the house he had been guarding, perhaps satisfied that his appearance alone had discouraged a two-legged prowler.

Twenty yards north of the corrals across the alley where Kelly kept a few horses, a coon-footed *grulla* mare as ugly as original sin leaned on the corral stringers, ears forward, watching the rear opening of the livery barn. Two more horses lined up beside her to do the same thing; whatever they were staring at was in the barn's dirt-floored runway. Walt's initial speculation was that since it was about feeding time, the horses were waiting for someone to pitch hay to them. The reason he began to doubt this was because horses watching someone inside a barn at feeding time usually nickered with impatience. When he was less than ten yards from them he could see three mounds of hay in their corral. They had already been fed, so it was not hunger that had attracted them.

He crept closer, paused to listen, eased another couple of yards, and halted when a man's deep, growly voice came distinctly from inside the barn. "The next time, you old son of a bitch, I'll break you neck. Now get over there and set down."

Walt groped for Jim McGregor's six-gun and stepped against the rough sidewall of the barn to open the little gate and turn the cylinder to satisfy himself the gun was fully loaded. Then he paused long enough to take down a couple of deep breaths before moving back into the alley. Now all the horses in the corral opposite the barn's rear opening were lined up, staring at whatever intrigued them up the runway.

Walt flattened alongside the rear wall, heard some kind of activity, and wished now that he had brought Fred down here with him, to stand watch out front.

A voice Walt recognized the moment he heard it said, "Herman, never mind the damned bridle. It don't have to fit good, just as long as the bit won't fall out."

The growly voice came again. "You ride your way an' I'll ride my way. Besides, there wasn't no one back there."

Walt shifted McGregor's gun to his left hand, ran his right palm down a trouser leg to rid it of sweat, and shifted it back. The *grulla* mare and her friends were ignoring him. Whatever the men were doing in the runway held their total interest. Walt hoped the men inside were equally as preoccupied as he measured the distance, then took two wide steps, and came around into full view of the barn's interior. He had two seconds to recognize old Bellingham sitting slumped on a wall bench holding one hand to his bloody mouth where he had been struck hard, and another two seconds to see Warren standing aside waiting impatiently for Herman Smith to finish adjusting the cheekpieces of a bridle so that the bit fit the saddled big rawboned brown horse he was holding.

Smith was leaning. From the corner of his eye he caught sight of sudden movement in the alley and lifted his head at the same time Walt cocked McGregor's handgun and raised it. Smith froze.

The larger man, who had been watching Smith, stiffened with abrupt alarm at the look on Smith's face. He had already been tense and fidgety. He dropped the reins to the horse he had been holding and spun with surprising speed for a man of his size and heft. His right hand was streaking for the handgun holster low on his right hip when Walt yelled at him.

"Hold it!"

He might as well have yelled at a stone wall. Warren completed his draw, and he was very fast. Walt shot him from a distance of about forty feet, and when the slug hit, it punched Warren against the horse he had been holding. The horse grunted in surprise and shied violently, striking the other saddled animal. Herman Smith was jostled off-balance as he too was reaching toward his holster.

Smith and Walt fired at about the same time. Smith missed by a yard because he was staggering when he tugged the trigger. Walt missed, but by a much smaller margin, because Warren was struggling to control the horse he had fallen against, which was a distraction.

Smith regained his stance as Walt sprang sideways. Behind him those corralled horses were stampeding in circles inside their pole corral. Smith fired, shattered a cedar post inside the corral, and was frantically thumbing the hammer back for his third shot when Walt took deliberate aim and squeezed the trigger.

Smith's hat sprang into the air like an injured bird and landed fifteen feet away, on the bench where Frank Bellingham had been sitting. There was no sign of Frank. He had jumped up to dive inside the harness-room at the first gunshot.

Herman Smith's eyes turned aimlessly. He had been too tense to fall easily, but as slackness set in, he went down, first to his knees, then pitched forward onto his face, shot squarely through the breastbone, dead before he stopped moving.

Warren pulled himself astride the frightened horse he had recaught and was hauling him around with his right hand locked short-up on the reins in a frantic grip. His left arm hung limply.

Constable Cutler turned from Smith. Warren had his horse aimed for the front barn opening as he sank in the spurs. The horse gave a mighty leap at the exact moment Walt fired. The bullet made a clean miss.

As Walt was dragging the hammer back for another shot, Warren sailed past the harness-room door and was within ten feet of breaking clear of the barn when old Bellingham sprang up into the doorway, stepped past it with his right arm rising. He called out: "You son of a bitch," and tugged the trigger of a handgun with a ten-inch barrel. White smoke billowed, the muzzle blast was deafening, and the big old gun's recoil hurled Frank's arm straight up above his head.

The slug that struck Warren was a thumb-sized lead ball, not a pointed bullet. At that distance the impact was roughly the equivalent of someone being struck head-on with a sledgehammer. Warren was lifted and hurled sideways from his saddle. His horse tucked up behind and hunched forward, leaving Mr. Warren in the air as he fell. The horse turned left and went racing in wild-eyed panic northward up through town.

Walt's ears were ringing, and the black-powder smoke from Frank Bellingham's old gun spread widely, with no air to move it very much. It had a decidedly unpleasant, sharp odor.

Walt put McGregor's gun up slowly and watched Frank Bellingham shuffle over and halt, staring down at Warren, whose shirt-front was turning lethally scarlet. Through diminishing echoes Walt heard the old man repeat what he had said before.

"You son of a bitch!"

Somewhere northward out in the roadway a man's outcry arose through dying echoes inside the livery barn. The sudden roar of gunfire at the lower end of town had startled the hell out of him.

Walt blew out a shaky breath and walked up the runway toward Frank Bellingham. The old man turned slowly, met Walt's solemn gaze, and raised his left hand to his lips. "I owed him that, Constable."

Walt nodded, looked at the dead man, then raised his eyes. "I thought you were in the jailhouse, Frank."

"No. The ladies let me come down to feed the horses. When O'Bryon left there was no one to do it." Bellingham raised his old gun, looked at it, then shoved it into the waistband of his trousers, and made an old soldier's joke without even a hint of humor in his eyes. "If it goes off I'll be singin' falsetto for the rest of my life . . . Walt?"

"Yes."

"I sure need a drink. That other one knocked me down when I told 'em to get the hell out of the barn."

Walt nodded again. "I need one too, Frank."

". . . But I'm not goin' to have one . . . I'd sure like some black coffee, though."

"All right, let's get some black coffee."

The sound of horses in the roadway made both men turn. Fred Tower rode up leading the horse Warren had tried to escape on. As he swung to the ground and glanced at the two dead men, he led the horses down into the runway, eyed Bellingham, the saw-handle grip of the big, old gun in his waistband, and he smiled. "You settle up for your pup, Frank?"

"Yes, sir."

Fred eyed them both. "Either one of you get hurt?"

Walt answered. "No. Scared peeless but I guess that's about all."

Fred looked again at the dead men, and in an offhand manner he said, "You should have kept one of 'em alive . . . Did they have any of the bullion with them?"

Walt resisted an urge to look at Warren when he replied. "No. But I know where it is."

Fred's head snapped up. Walt did not elaborate. He took Frank Bellingham by the arm and started up out of the barn with him, leaving Fred to care for the horses.

At the jailhouse he had to light the office lamp. Dusk had settled, and darkness was coming. It was still warm, but regardless of that Walt poked kindling into the stove, got a little fire going, and put his coffeepot atop the stove.

Bellingham was sitting on a wall bench with his old gun lying beside him. He could not have sat down with that ten-inch barrel in the front of his britches. He looked up at Walt. "I never thought I'd see that man again. When he and that other one came into the barn while I was hanging up the pitchfork, I couldn't believe my eyes. They went after horses and outfits like I wasn't standing there. When you've lived the way I've lived, for as long as I've lived, you can smell bad trouble. That husky one hit me in the mouth. I'll say one thing for him—he could hit like a mule kick."

Walt put two cups on the edge of the desk and left Frank in the office while he went down into his cell-room. Jack Pinter was lying out full length on his wall bunk and sat up very slowly, staring at the filthy, unshaven, rumpled, sunken-eyed man looking in at him.

Walt entered the cell, pulled up its only piece of furniture, a small stool, and sat down. When Pinter swung to the edge of the bunk, Walt leveled a finger at him. "Stay right there. Don't get up." He lowered his hand. "I want you to tell me something . . ."

Pinter interrupted. "What was all that shootin' about?"

Walt ignored the question. "I want a straight answer from you, Pinter. You said they left you behind to turn all the livery horses loose if it looked to you like I was going to make up a posse."

The muscular, large man with the too-small head nodded. "That's right."

"Maybe that's right as far as it went. Now I want you to tell me what else you were supposed to do."

Pinter blinked. "What else?"

"Yeah . . . You remember what can happen to a prisoner trying to escape? Walt lifted out McGregor's gun and aimed it without cocking it. "What else?"

Pinter licked his lips, glanced in the direction of the shadowy little dingy corridor, then glanced back again. "Give 'em two days, then ride up north with saddle horses for them."

"Where, Pinter?"

Well, ride around up near them foothills until I saw the wagon. There wouldn't be no trouble seeing something like that."

Walt slowly holstered McGregor's gun. "You did pretty well. Now then, let's try something else. You'd ride one horse up there and lead two?"

"No. One for Buck, one for Herman, an' one for Mr. Warren."

"Then the four of you would abandon the wagons and ride for it?"

"That's right."

"You are forgetting something, Jack. About two tons of gold and silver bars. There'd be no way you could move even a tenth of that kind of weight on four saddle horses."

Pinter gripped the edge of the bunk and rocked slightly back and forth before saying, "I've told you everything I'm goin' to. . . . Go ahead and shoot me, but that's all."

Walt thinly smiled at the younger man. "All right, Jack," he said, and arose to go stand in the doorway before turning back, no longer smiling. "You been helpful. Now I'll be the same . . . Buck Jensen is dead, crushed when the floorboards of one of your wagons opened while he was underneath it. The bullion crushed him flat. Warren and Herman Smith are down in the livery barn, shot to death. That's what all the gunfire was about."

Pinter was motionless on the edge of the bunk, staring.

Walt stepped out of the cell, closed the door, swung the brass lock closed, snapped it, and leaned on the door looking in. "A man from the mining company down south came out with the posse from town to take over the rig that killed Jensen. By now he'll be driving back to town with the rig— and the bullion bars. . . . Jack, you're the only one still alive so it's up to you—when you and the others rode around the country with Warren looking for a decent way through— that's not what you were lookin' for, is it?"

Pinter did not make a sound. He was staring at Walt without blinking.

"Warren took you fellers with him to help him find a hiding place for those bars of gold and silver, and you found it. The plan was to cache the bullion, abandon the wagons, and get out of the country and come back, maybe next year in the night, and get the loot. Jack, the harnessmaker, and I found that second wagon after Warren and Smith abandoned it and rode for town to steal a pair of saddle horses to get away on. . . . The wagon was empty. What you better tell me is where exactly that cache is, because if you don't you're goin' to have the damndest accident you can imagine, and it won't be here in my jailhouse; it'll be somewhere up near the foothills where you ran to before I caught up and killed you.

"Where is the cache, Jack? You can help by telling me because we'll find it anyway. It'll just be quicker if you tell me. Otherwise we're goin' to have to waste weeks poking around in that lava-rock country." Walt nodded and returned to the jailhouse office where Frank Bellingham was drinking black coffee and looking perfectly normal.

He eyed Constable Cutler and pointed to a cup on the edge of the desk. "Did you tell him what happened down in the barn?"

Walt sat down at his desk with the coffee cup. "Yeah, among other things. Now he can sit down there in the dark deciding whether he wants to get maybe five years in prison or a headstone. He's got until morning to make up his mind." Walt tasted the coffee. It was much better than he was accustomed to. "You make good java, Frank."

Bellingham arose to get a refill. "I didn't make it, Miz Maloney did." He thought of something and looked at his clothes. There was blood on them. "She's goin' to raise cain. She told me to keep my clothes clean . . . She isn't going to like this."

Fred walked in, tugging his gloves off as he kicked the door closed behind himself. He went straight to the coffee-pot, filled a cup, and turned with his back to the stove. "I drug them into a stall and covered them with a wagon-canvas." He tasted the coffee, then emptied the cup without pausing, and turned to refill it. "Did you make this coffee, Frank? Best I've tasted in—"

"I didn't make it, Miz Maloney did."

Fred's hands stopped for five seconds, then resumed what they had been doing. As he turned this time with a cupful he shot a glance in Walt's direction.

Walt looked at him and shrugged. "She's good at cooking too," he murmured, gazing into the cup he was cradling between both hands.

Fred sipped his coffee while gazing at the door. When he

had emptied the cup he put it aside and walked to the door as he said, "Now, by Gawd, I'm going to sleep for a week, then maybe eat five times a day for another week, and—"

Walt interrupted. "I'll meet you at the livery barn in the morning. We're going to take that prisoner I got up to the foothills, and he's going to show us where Warren's cache is."

Fred's brows dropped a notch. "Is that what they done with it—hid it up there?"

"It's all they could have done with it, Fred. Nothing else fits. What we found was an empty wagon, and they didn't have any of it with them when they got shot."

The harnessmaker looked at the floor for a long moment before grasping the door latch and squeezing it. Then he said, "And that will end it?"

Walt nodded his head. "Mostly."

"No. Now didn't give me that 'mostly' idea. That will end it."

"Well, as far as you're concerned it will, but I've got to take the man from the mining company up there, find those horses, get them back on the war wagon we left up there, and after that it's up to him how he gets it all loaded and hauled back down to Gloria."

Fred opened the door halfway. "While you're with that gent, Walt, you might want to mention that thousand dollars Kelly and me figure his company owes us."

Walt pushed his empty cup aside. "I'll tell him. Go home and get some sleep. I'll see you in the morning."

After the door closed, Walt arose to sink his cup, and the one Fred had left, into a bucket of oily water he kept behind the stove. As he turned, Frank Bellingham stood up to sink his cup too and said, "I expect I can get a room up at Miz Maloney's place."

Walt regarded the tall, gaunt old man, his expression thoughtful. Bellingham misinterpreted the look and added, "She told me to come up, Constable. I'll find work and pay her."

Walt nodded, waited until Bellingham was outside, then

blew down the lamp mantle and joined him on the plankwalk. He locked the jailhouse from the outside. As they were walking northward he was thinking of maybe a third of the one-thousand-dollar reward going to the old man; after all, Frank Bellingham was the man who had stopped the outlaw who had robbed the mining company from escaping; they ought to be grateful for that. The question was just how grateful? Even a few hundred dollars would help. Frank had his self-respect back, he had settled his score with an outlaw, and Walt had no intention of just abandoning him now that he was working his way back.

The old man suddenly looked up from beneath tufted eyebrows. "Is Mr. Tower sweet on Miz Maloney?"

Walt cleared his throat. "Well, they're right good friends."

Bellingham walked a few feet before speaking again. "She's a fine woman, Constable. Strong as oak, and that means alot in a female, if they use a little cleverness along with it . . . My wife was that way. After a few years when I got to knowing how she managed things so well without making me mad, I used to laugh to myself about it . . . Constable, I don't believe there are too many women still around that got that kind of wisdom. Do you?"

Walt was looking at the darkened front window of Elizabeth Bartlett's cafe when he answered. "I don't know, Frank, but one of these days I'm going to find out."

The last thing he heard before entering the dark rooming house was the faint and muted rumble of a very heavy wagon somewhere southward, probably in the vicinity of Kelly O'Bryon's barn. He was tired enough to ignore it.

CHAPTER 24
Solving Problems

JACK PINTER had reached his decision long before Constable Cutler appeared at the jailhouse in the pale, chilly dawn. He was waiting when Walt entered the cell-room and looked in at him. "You ready to ride?" Pinter asked, and Walt unlocked the door without speaking, jerked his head, and followed Pinter up to the office. There, with his prisoner watching, he took a booted Winchester from the rack and herded Pinter outside and southward with the weapon in the crook of one arm.

Fred Tower was waiting, looking bleary-eyed but freshly scrubbed and shaved. Beside him was the mine official, a big man with a droopy moustache. His black coat, hat, and britches were layered with dust as he nodded to Constable Cutler. Fred said, "I met him last night when he come through town with the wagon. Told him in case you didn't see him to meet us down here."

Kelly O'Bryon was also up and stirring, although he did not seem to have been awake very long. He was rigging out three horses in the runway and barely grunted as the men who would be riding them walked down there. When he was finished, though, he did make one concession: he jerked his head in the direction of the harness-room and said, "Coffee's hot, gents, since you ain't going to get any breakfast."

They trooped into the smelly little room, waited for Kelly to fill several tin cups, then stood like mutes. Kelly was eyeing Walt before the cups were emptied. "I still got to have a hostler," he said, and waited for the response which did not come before saying the rest of it. "I'd like to get old Bellingham back, Walt. At least until I can find another man."

Walt put down his emptied cup. "Just for today, Kelly. Just until I get back. That'll give you plenty of time to find someone."

Kelly accepted that. It was more than he had expected. "Where are you fellers going with Pinter?"

Walt turned toward the door as he said, "Horseback riding," and went along to free the reins to the horse he would ride and lead it outside before mounting.

He did not tie Pinter's hands or drop a rope around the neck of his horse, so anyone watching the quartet leave town in the cold pre-dawn would assume it was a congenial foursome. But it was improbable that anyone who might be looking out would be very interested.

Trent, the mine official, made a point of riding beside Jack Pinter. Pinter, who'd had six or seven hours to understand his position—he was the only one of Warren's immediate party still alive—was gloomily cooperative. He told Trent details of the Warren conspiracy that even Constable Cutler did not know, but by the time the sun was a hidden streamer of gold against the farthest side of the eastward mountains, the details were less important than the destination of the party.

Fred rode behind with Constable Cutler. He had seemed preoccupied even before leaving Peralta. With sunlight suddenly flooding the world, without warmth yet, he pulled off his gloves, stuffed them under his shellbelt, and felt through his pockets for the fresh plug he had taken from a drawer at the harness shop. As he was slicing off a corner with a razor-sharp Barlow knife, he said, "You sleep good last night, Constable?"

Walt had indeed slept well. "Like a dead man. You?"

Fred got his chew into position before replying. He was gazing up ahead, where it was possible to make out jumbles of those pockmarked boulders. "Yeah, I slept well. Only it was a time before I dropped off."

Walt nodded about that. It was common for tired people to

be unable to drop off immediately. He had no idea Fred was leading up to something, but when he said nothing the harnessmaker sighed loudly.

"There was a piece of paper slid under the door of the shop. If it hadn't been white I wouldn't have seen it in the dark."

Walt turned to eye his friend.

"It was from Miz Maloney."

Walt's interest heightened a little but he still kept silent.

". . . Something to do with a picnic."

The constable began to have a premonition. With elaborate unconcern he said, "What is today, Fred?"

"Saturday."

Walt looked up ahead. They were passing the first of those lavender-brown rocks with the little shallow holes all over them. "What about the picnic?" he asked.

"Well, I thought maybe you'd know. Bertha and Elizabeth Bartlett got it organized. They fetch the grub. It will be them, you an' me and Frank Bellingham."

Walt rode five yards staring at the brilliantly revealed and very distant mountain rims. The distance was not less than forty miles, yet he could make out individual trees up there, even the limbs of individual trees.

He had known Frank Bellingham would be along. He'd had no idea Bertha or Fred would. He did not feel especially annoyed, but he felt *something* because the last time he and Elizabeth had been alone together it had been tantalizingly worrisome to him, and he'd had reason to expect something more personal would arise the next time they were together—except that, hell's fire, not with half the confounded town of Peralta at the picnic too.

"It ought to be a good dinner," he said impassively.

Fred nodded, still looking up ahead as the mine company's man twisted in the saddle to ask where they should leave the road. Neither Walt nor Fred replied. Jack Pinter did by raising an arm and leading the way.

Pinter was straightening from a slouch when Walt's growl settled him back down in the saddle. "Just walk your horse. We're not goin' to a fire."

He obeyed, his expression sullen. If he'd had any thoughts of trying to make a run for it, they must have been influenced by something a man of his background would certainly realize—there had never been a horse foaled who could outrun bullets.

He led them unerringly to one of those building-high jumbles of lava-rock. Walt and Fred studied the ground. They had loped past this exact spot yesterday in their haste to overtake the wagon, and they had not been looking at the ground, but even if they had been, they might have been lulled because someone had expertly dragged out the sign.

Where Pinter stopped, off to the side of the road, there was a large pile of boulders. He jutted his chin. "That's the place we decided on when Lightle led us all over hell tryin' to find the right place to hide the loot." Pinter shook his head in dour recollection. "We must have passed up a dozen spots as good as this one before he was satisfied. We dug a big hole, then covered it with slats of wood and rocks. The plan was they'd drive off the road here and release the belly-dumps. After all the bullion was hid, they'd cover the hole again and hide the wagons."

Fred remained with the prisoner. Walt and Trent dismounted and walked closer to the huge rockpile. Walt was leery but Trent began moving boulders aside until he could see the wooden planks. Then Walt helped him remove the rest of the rocks and lift off a plank.

Walt got belly-down on a plank. Trent balanced on some rocks at the edge of the hole, using his hands to support himself as he spoke across the open place to Walt, without looking away from the bullion. "It was an ideal place. The only things that might see his cache would be worms and chucks." Trent finally looked across at Constable Cutler. "Where is the wagon?"

Walt gestured. "A mile or so northeast of here. I got no idea where the horses are. There was only two of them on the pole anyway. We turned 'em loose, but they'll be around." As Trent nodded, Walt added a little more. "You can't move this cache with two horses. Kelly O'Bryon can fix you up with two more."

Trent raised his hat to mop sweat which was only just beginning and probably not from morning heat because it really was not that hot yet, when Walt looked directly at him as he spoke again. "I never tried conducting business while balancin' atop a mound of rocks before, but there's something else, Trent."

"What else? You can take me to the wagon, we can find the horses, and I can rent another pair from O'Bryon—and down below is what I came up here for."

"Well, Mr. Trent, there is the matter of several men making it possible for you to get your gold and silver back."

The big man stared across the distance. ". . . Constable, I'm already shy one gold bar. The company I work for doesn't make a business of—"

"Mister Trent," said Walt a trifle sharply as he cut across the other man's words. "Kelly O'Bryon and Fred Tower took a chance on getting killed to find your damned bullion for you. If it'd been just up to you, I don't think you'd ever have found it. Sure as hell not this pile of it . . . I'm talkin' about a recovery reward. How much is all this bullion worth—this pile and the load you brought back to town last night?"

Trent was getting red in the face. "I don't know exactly how much, Constable, but—"

"Maybe a couple hundred thousand dollars, Mr. Trent? I'm asking for your word that you'll see that your company sends one thousand dollars to both O'Bryon and Tower . . . and then there's Frank Bellingham, the man who killed Warren, or whatever you want to call him. Frank made damned sure your company won't ever be robbed by Warren again. He also stopped him from escaping, an' if Warren had got away, I doubt like hell that you or the law could have caught him before he got down over the line into Mexico."

Trent gingerly shifted his position and glared down at the mound of bullion bars. "Three thousand dollars?" he asked angrily.

"That sure is a big pile of gold and silver down there, isn't it, Mr. Trent? Let me ask you something: would your company be willing to pay three thousand dollars to buy a pile like that?"

Trent did not respond. He turned and very carefully began climbing over the boulders to the ground. As he was dusting himself off, Constable Cutler came striding around from the other side of the hole. "Wouldn't you figure that'd be a real bargain, several hundred thousand dollars worth of gold and silver for only three thousand dollars, Mr. Trent?"

The unsmiling company man looked stonily at Constable Cutler. "It won't be just three thousand," he replied. "It will be closer to nine, Constable, because of that bar you gave those Mexicans."

Walt nodded his head. "Still, one hell of a bargain. Now, let's go find the wagon and see where the horses got to."

The wagon was where it had been abandoned, but the team horses were nowhere in sight. Trent would never find them.

There was heat before the horsemen got back to town. Trent did not shed his black Prince Albert coat. No one in Peralta had seen him without it. But the men he had ridden north with had not only shed their coats, they had tied them behind their cantles out of the way, to allow any vagrant breeze which might come along to dry their sweat and cool them off.

As they were helping Kelly and Frank Bellingham off-saddle in the cool runway, Trent inquired about hiring four big, strong draft horses and perhaps a driver for the second wagon. Kelly said nothing until he had taken an outfit into the harness-room to be draped from a wall peg and returned, "I got the horses," he said, "but you want to be almighty careful about who you hire to drive one of them wagons. There's already been folks pokin' around that other one you parked across the alley last night. Frank and I been busy as bees chasin' them off—but Mr. Trent, something like bullion can't be kept a secret very long."

Trent said, "All right, just find me a driver. As for the rest of it, don't fret, Mr. O'Bryon, I'll send down to the mine for ten armed men to meet me on the road to Gloria."

Kelly turned toward Fred Tower. The harnessmaker looked back, first in surprise, then in darkening anger. "No, you don't, Kelly. Not on your life would I drive one of them wagons . . . You just waltz up to the Horseshoe Saloon and put your schemin' head beside the connivin' head of Pat Flannery. The two of you can come up with someone." Fred stamped out of the barn and was still indignant by the time he reached the coolness of his shop.

Constable Cutler shook hands with the mining company man. "About those finder's fees," Walt said.

Trent looked almost mournful when he answered. "I'll tell you something I thought about on the ride back, Constable . . . If we ever get pirated again, so help me Gawd it can be in any direction but north to the Peralta country. You gents are worse'n bandits."

Walt smiled straight at the man with the droopy moustache. "I sure don't want to argue with you, but I got to tell you that I sure don't have a guilty conscience. Three thousand for the three men who did the most to save your bullion and wipe out the men who sure as hell would have raided you again?"

"And what about you, Constable; another thousand?"

"No. Nothing for me, Mr. Trent."

The man dressed all in black looked speculatively at Walt. "All right; on one condition. You help me guard the wagons until I get under way in the morning."

Walt hesitated. "I can't help you tonight, and I've got something else I got to do tomorrow."

Trent looked more annoyed than disappointed, until Kelly

volunteered to help guard the wagons. Then Walt prodded his prisoner and left the barn.

Up at the jailhouse he locked Pinter into his cell, went over to the cafe for pails of food, and Elizabeth greeted him with a shy, inquisitive smile. He told her he would have a wagon for the picnic by morning, and returned to feed his prisoner. After that he went up to the rooming house, went out to the bathhouse to take an all-over bath, and on his way back to his room encountered Bertha Maloney, who blushed when they met, which surprised Cutler; he could not recall ever having seen Bertha blush before. She told him she had heard some of the details of his recent difficulty, and he promised to tell her the rest of them at the picnic tomorrow. Then he went to his room to sleep until late evening.

She turned back several men, among them Jim McGregor from the bank, who wanted answers to a number of questions. Shortly before dusk, when Walt appeared in the hallway, Bertha was dusting her parlor and intercepted him near the roadway door. She blushed again and considered the feathers in her duster instead of looking at him when she asked if Fred Tower had come back to town without injury.

He assured her that Fred was probably better off from his exercise than he would have been if he had not left the shop, and waited for whatever she had to say next, because it was obvious that something else was on her mind.

While still examining the duster she asked a question. "By any chance, Constable, did he mention me while you were with him out yonder?"

Walt considered his answer carefully. "He said something about you, Bertha, only I don't exactly remember what it was. We were kind of busy out there."

Her eyes finally came up to his face. "Did Elizabeth tell you that Fred and I'll be along on the picnic tomorrow?"

He knew they would be along but Elizabeth hadn't told him. "No. But it'll be nice if you two are along . . . Bertha?"

"Yes."

"Fred's . . . I don't think he's been around women very much." She was watching him closely, which added to the difficulty of what he was trying to say. "I guess you and Fred been friends for a long time."

"Yes, we have, Constable . . . I . . . Elizabeth and I talked while you and Fred were out yonder."

"About Fred?"

"Well, not just about Fred. About you too."

Walt had lost the initiative and was not aware of it and at this moment he would not have cared anyway. "I'll tell you straight out, Bertha; I thought when this picnic idea came up it would be just Elizabeth and me."

Bertha nodded her head as though this did not surprise her. "I think Elizabeth had the same notion, then she got to feeling sorry for Frank Bellingham. Constable—it's time. It's time for you to . . . Do you mind if I ask you a personal question straight out?"

"No."

"Did you have in mind setting a date when to get married? At the picnic tomorrow?"

"Kind of hard to do with half the town around, Bertha."

"No, it isn't. I'll keep Frank and Fred away. You just take her for a little walk. But you didn't answer my question."

"Yes'm, I had something like that in mind."

Bertha's hard eyes were soft. "It's time, Constable."

"You're sure? How do you know?"

Bertha considered the feather duster again and replied in a very quiet tone of voice. "We talked. Like I said, we talked about Fred and you. She's right fond of you. I told her the pair of you belong together."

"Bertha?"

"She agreed, Constable . . . I got to get a new duster, look at these ragged old feathers."

"Bertha!"

"I took a long chance, Constable . . . I told her you'd maybe want to set the date tomorrow."

"What did she say?"

". . . She said she hoped you would."

Walt gazed at the sturdy, graying woman, then leaned and kissed her cheek and walked out onto the rooming-house porch. There was dust in the roadway where several horsemen had just passed heading northward up out of town. Through the dust he saw Fred Tower emerge from the cafe sucking his teeth. Fred was wearing a new pair of britches and a new white shirt. He walked southward to intercept the harnessmaker outside of his shop. He looked him up and down, then said, "You look mighty decent for a change."

Fred looked down his nose with a suspicious stare. "A man's got a right to spruce up. Did you talk to that feller with the droopy moustache who dresses like an undertaker?"

"Yeah. He agreed. A thousand dollars for you and Kelly— and for Frank Bellingham."

Fred's eyes widened. "Frank too? Did you use a gun?"

"No . . . About the picnic tomorrow, Fred . . ."

"What about it? They called it off?"

"No. I was thinkin' about Bertha."

Fred's eyes slid away, found a knot in the plankwalk, and remained fixed on it. "I been thinkin' about her too, Walt. You'n me been good friends a long time."

"Most likely always will be, Fred"

"Well, maybe not if you dragoon me into any more of your consarned messes. But, about Bertha . . ."

"Go ahead, spit it out, Fred."

"Like I just said, I been thinkin' about her."

"That's nothing new. Get on with it."

Tower's gaze returned to the lawman's face. "I don't want to get her mad at me."

Walt sighed; this was like pulling teeth. "You're not going to make Bertha mad."

Fred was silent for a moment while studying the face of his friend. "You don't know what I was fixing to say."

"Yes I do, but the way you're goin' about it, it'll be dark again before you say it."

"Walt, I never been married, an' I chew, an' I'm old, an' I'm—"

"Fred, she won't be carrying a gun, and she can't catch you in a footrace, so just up and ask her."

Fred's gaze sparked. "In front of you'n old Frank Bellingham and Miz Bartlett?"

"No, damn it, after we eat, just take her for a little stroll. When you're out a ways just say it straight out."

"And suppose I make her mad an' she turns me down?"

"She is not going to get mad or turn you down."

Fred stood there a moment or two, then glanced into his shop through the front window. "Are you plumb sure of that?"

"I'd bet my life on it, Fred." Walt slapped the harnessmaker on the arm and started on over in the direction of the cafe. He was hungry. Not as hungry as he had a right to be after missing a few meals the last couple of days, but hungry anyway. Even if he hadn't been, the cafe drew him toward it like a magnet.

If you have enjoyed this book and would like to receive details of other Walker Western titles, please write to:

Western Editor
Walker and Company
720 Fifth Avenue
New York, NY 10019